WE COULD BE BROTHERS

DERRICK BARNES

WE COULD BE BROTHERS

SCHOLASTIC INC.

New York Toronto London Auckland
Sydney Mexico City New Delhi Hong Kong

No part of this publication may be reproduced, stored in a retrieval system, or transmitted in any form or by any means, electronic, mechanical, photocopying, recording, or otherwise, without written permission of the publisher. For information regarding permission, write to Scholastic Inc., Attention: Permissions Department, 557 Broadway, New York, NY 10012.

ISBN 978-0-545-35797-5

Copyright © 2010 by Derrick Barnes.
All rights reserved. Published by Scholastic Inc.
SCHOLASTIC and associated logos are trademarks and/or registered trademarks of Scholastic Inc.

12 11 10 9 8 7 6 5 4 3 2 1   11 12 13 14 15 16/0

Printed in the U.S.A.   40

First Scholastic paperback printing, January 2011

The text type was set in Bookman Old Style.
The display type was set in DIN.
Book design by Whitney Lyle

For Dr. Alfred Tatum,
Associate Professor and Director of the
University of Illinois at Chicago Reading Clinic,
and to all of the young,
brilliant brother authors.
Continue to speak and write unapologetically.
— DB

STRANGERS ON TUESDAY

As soon as the bell rang, 2:30 on the dot, classroom doors swung wide open and we flew out into the hallways like we were shot from cannons. Mr. Monk's sixth-period social science class is a super-slow death. Each minute in that class feels more like five minutes. We hit up our lockers and came pouring down the main stairs from the second floor: a human waterfall, flowing fast — sixth, seventh, and eighth graders spilling across the Alain Locke school crest, flooding out the doorways.

Usually, I'm a part of all of that, but today was different. Today was so embarrassing, I didn't even tell my dad. I lied to him and told him that, for the next three days, I'd be staying after school to work on a science fair project.

Yeah, right. He'd be so disappointed if he knew the truth.

All day I thought about taking that long dreaded stroll down the Bermuda Hallway.

On the ground floor, right next to the boys' locker room, is a set of stairs that is so deep, so narrow, so musty and hot. There have been kids who've gone down but never came back up. It's a stupid school legend that I can't say is true or not, and I was not looking forward to finding out.

There are some kids that travel the Bermuda Hallway like they do the daily path to their own homeroom. That ain't me, but I guess it'll be me for the next three days.

As soon as I walked through the raggedy, darkened doorway, the noise behind me got muffled. The laughing, the arguing, and the cussing slowly began to fade until I heard nothing but my own footsteps.

There were lights along the walls of the stairwell that flickered like somebody'd forgotten to pay the electric bill. The farther I went, the more I felt like a part of the underworld that is PSS — Post-School Suspension.

Principal Richmond refuses to waste any valuable time during a regular school day to punish students. He is the originator, the god-father, the evil scientist behind the invention of PSS. Anytime a student gets into trouble, they'll be punished on their own time. That means sacrificing those sweet valuable hours right after school lets out. Principal Richmond knows that we'd rather be at home, continuing the game we've saved on Madden, raiding the fridge and making our mothers upset by snacking before dinner, or just chillin'. Being at school, in the basement, after school lets out? That's so whack, it's beyond even talking about. But hey, what can you do?

When I got to the bottom of the stairwell, I expected to see ashes, torn-up clothes, and the bones of kids who never made it out alive. A bunch of tubes and pipes hung above me, some metal, some plastic, some rusted. They leaked in spots, and flushed, rattled, and whined in others. Soon the lights stopped flickering, and dimmed for good.

At the end of the hallway, music seeped from underneath the PSS room door. I couldn't make out what kind of music it was. All I heard were muffled sounds. No talking, just suffocated noise.

A sign made of a copper-wired frame hung

eye level next to the door. You can't miss it. Encased in the frame was a quote from Frederick Douglass for all who entered the godforsaken place to read:

People might not get all they work for in this world, but they must certainly work for all they get.

I gave the door a tiny shove. It screeched open like an angry crow. Before I even walked inside, I heard the music crystal clear. It was "People Make the World Go 'Round" from an old-school group called the Stylistics, my dad's favorite group.

A bearded man with a large barrel-shaped gut stood up from his desk, with a weird and unexpected smile. "Come on in, son. I think you're the last one."

I stepped in, dejected and ready to face my punishment like a man.

"Please, son, don't come in late again," said the grinning lumberjack PSS teacher. Both of his thumbs were trapped under his striped suspenders. All he needed was a pipe in his mouth. He looked like he was ready to eat a plate full of flapjacks or cut down a few trees.

"My name is Patt," he said. "*Mr.* Patt." He squeezed around his desk and stood in front of it, covering up the whole thing. Then he cleared his throat and continued. "Look, I only have one serious rule for you to follow — do the work we've provided for you. You can stay for three days or for the remainder of the month. It's all up to me."

The "work we've provided for you" was filing, stapling, and collating hundreds of papers. On top of doing this PSS thing every day after school,

I'd still have to go home and do my homework. That was messed up.

Mr. Patt returned to his desk, and I settled in at a worktable. There were only three other students serving time with me. At one table was a scrawny, chicken-necked kid with thick red hair. He was wearing his big brother's gear; everything seemed ten sizes too big, even his shoes. After finishing each stack of papers, he'd sneeze and then suck the snot back up into his nose. I thought kids stopped swallowing that stuff when they left elementary, but this guy proved me wrong. He had to be a sixth grader to do that kind of snorting. It was gross, even for a sixth grader.

Mr. Patt called over to the snot sucker, "Hey, Mackey — blow your nose, man! Nobody wants to hear that mess!"

Mackey giggled, then wiped his nose with one of his extra-large sleeves.

The only girl in the room, an eighth grader named Rosilyn I recognized from some of my classes, dropped her stapler at her workstation. She sighed real heavy and then switched her skinny self over to Mr. Patt's desk. She snatched up a big box of Kleenex. "Dang, boy! Why you gotta be so nasty? Uuuuuuh!" Rosilyn scolded Mackey like she was his mama.

Mr. Patt was glued to his computer. He bumped up the volume on his MacBook, then clicked REPEAT and gave the Stylistics another spin. Rosilyn threw the box of tissues at Mackey. He grabbed a couple and put them in his pocket, but kept right on wiping with his sleeves.

The other kid who was stuck with us in PSS also looked like an eighth grader. I didn't really know him, but I was pretty sure I'd had sixth- and seventh-grade classes with him. He sat with his back to all of us and acted like he was in the room by himself. He didn't even pay attention to Mr. Patt when he was running down the PSS rule. The cord from the kid's white iPod earbuds swung from his side. He swayed back and forth, mouthing lyrics like a muted MC.

He turned around once to mean-mug Rosilyn and the chicken-necked snot boy. There was a long keloid scar running from his left cheek to his chin. When I first saw him, I thought he *acted* like a kid who belonged in PSS — angry, a lot of attitude, and looking for a fight around every corner.

Mackey was stacking. Patt was caught up in

a sudoku online tournament. Rosilyn took a break from her stapling duties. She chewed and popped her gum all the way over to my station, where I was clipping permission slips together. She worked her gum like one of those waitresses at the Waffle House. Rosilyn leaned one hand on my table and placed the other one on a hip of her low-riding Apple Bottoms jeans. Still chewing, she looked me up and down and said, "What are *you* doin' down here? Ain't you in Mrs. Fariss's lit class with me? You always sit in the front, right?" I kept paper-clipping and nodded my head yes. She emptied the paper clips from the box and scattered them all over my table. "I know you ain't playing uppity with me! You can talk, right? What's your name anyway?" Rosilyn demanded.

"Robeson. My name is Robeson," I snapped at her. Rosilyn waved her hand in my face. I think she got a kick out of rubbing me the wrong way.

"So you never did say why you're with us in PSS."

"It's for something stupid. I don't even belong down here."

"Yeah, none of us do. I don't care. I'll be back in here next month. I don't *even* care!"

"Maybe *you* don't care, but I don't like wasting *my* time," I said.

Rosilyn rolled her eyes, took out her gum, and stuck it underneath my tabletop. She pranced over to the mean-mugging kid's station and tapped him on his shoulder. "Pacino. Pacino. PACINO CLAPTON!" The kid was ignoring her. "Let me get some of your staples, boy."

He yanked his earbuds out and turned around, lips curled, his fists balled up. "Don't you ever put your filthy hands on me!" he growled. "I don't want anybody to ever say they saw me and you close together. Get away. I ain't giving you anything!"

As much spice as Rosilyn had, I knew she had a comeback for this Pacino kid, but she kept quiet. She rolled her eyes and slumped back to her seat, looking defeated already.

Mackey, the snotty sixth grader, snickered. Mr. Patt never looked up from his laptop. He just mumbled, "Hey-hey-hey. Keep it down."

That was it. Nobody cared about Pacino's sharp words, which had sliced through the air, snipped Rosilyn deep, and fallen hard at her feet. Pacino's earbuds were tucked in tight. He was back to bobbing his head.

Who was this kid? I'd only seen him once or twice. But I couldn't just let his attitude slide. I really wanted to know what his problem was. Maybe I was just frustrated about being in PSS. Maybe it was stupidity. Something made me step to him.

I picked up the paper clips Rosilyn had emptied out on my table, took a hard breath, and walked over to Pacino's station. He was taller than me, but definitely skinnier. I knew he was going to try to jump bad with me, but I didn't care. Somebody had to talk to this guy.

I tapped him on his shoulder. He turned around and yelled, "Look, girl, I told you to —" When he saw it was me, he stopped quick. He yanked out one earbud, curled his lips again, and said, "Man, . . . what you want?" He looked me up and down like I was a peon.

"I just . . . I just . . . What's up with you and Rosilyn?" I asked.

"Why? Do you want her? You can have her. She ain't nothing to me. She's been with everybody in the school anyway," he said.

"Do you know that for sure?" I asked.

"Man, . . . look at how she dresses. She's just asking for it."

"But you don't know for sure that she's been with everybody in the school, right?"

"I don't know who she messes around with, but I do know *I* don't want her. Anyway, why do you care what I say about her?" Pacino asked. He gave me a mug so mean it would scare at least ten women shopping on the Plaza.

I said, "I don't even know the girl. It just seemed jacked up that she would let you snap on her like that. You know what I'm saying?"

Mackey finally looked up. He muttered, "Uh-oh."

Rosilyn smiled at me and shook her head at the same time. She gave me a look like I should have kept my mouth shut.

Pacino tugged the other earbud out and then set his iPod on the table. Both of his fists were clenched. He lunged at me, but I didn't move an inch. I wasn't going to let him punk me like that.

He noticed that I wasn't sweating his thug act. He said, "So what you want? I mean, you think I disrespected your girl and everything? What's up?"

I braced myself. "Would you talk to your mama or sister like that?"

"What you just say? My mama? Man, don't ask me about my mama! You don't know me like that, fool. Rosilyn knows I was just playing with her. She just needs to back up off of me," Pacino growled. Then he pushed his pointer finger smack dead between my eyes. "Look, playboy, we got two more days down here. Unless you want to start wearing false teeth, you better stay over there. The only reason I haven't popped you in your grille is because I don't want to spend any more time than I have to in this hole. *That's* what's up!"

Rosilyn looked at me again and gave me the eyes of a damsel being shielded from the fiery breath of a dragon. Mackey wiped his runny nose on his sleeve. Filthy sixth grader.

Pacino went back to mean-mugging me, but I ignored him. For some reason, because my pants weren't sagging to the floor like his and I didn't keep a mean look on my face, he must've thought I was soft. He shook his head at me like I was about to be sorry for something.

Two days left in PSS.

I figured if I just did what I was in PSS to do —
collate and clip at *my* station — the time would
go faster.

I stared straight ahead at the wall. Well, not
actually the wall but at an ancient Michael
Jordan "Reading Is Fundamental" poster that
was so old, Jordan had hair.

Just when I was about to collate my last big
stack, a finger as sharp as an ice pick tapped
me on my shoulder. It was Pacino.

"I just don't get it," he said. "I've been over
there crammin' to understand why you would
take up for that girl when you don't even know
her." Pacino stood next to me, pretending to collate so that Mr. Patt wouldn't say anything. "I
mean . . . fools get knocked out for dumb stuff
like that."

"Hey, man, it's not just you. Even if it was Mackey or Mr. Patt, I would've said something." I was still staring straight ahead and organizing my stacks. We were standing a couple of feet apart, but I could feel Pacino looking at me, or through me, like I was made of glass.

"That's the type of thing you do for your moms or your sisters. I'm just sayin' . . . Rosilyn is used to people talking to her all crazy."

"I wouldn't be used to that," I said.

"Hey, she just stopped caring about stuff like that." Pacino looked over toward Rosilyn. She had her iPod, too; it was smaller, a red nano. I think she was checking out a new Rihanna video. She was tapping her fingernails on the table, looking lost in her own world.

I stopped fumbling with my papers and asked Pacino, "Whatever happened to respecting girls and all that stuff?"

"Man, first they need to earn respect. Besides, she knows I was just playin'." Pacino looked a little guilty. "And for real . . . if somebody talked bad to my moms, I'd beat him down so bad, his own folks wouldn't recognize him."

"That's what I'm talking about. I'd do the same thing," I agreed with Pacino.

"Man, . . . I know you ain't fightin' anybody."

"You don't even know me," I said.

"Don't worry about it." He skipped over the talk about fighting and went back to speaking about respect and stuff. "But I feel you, though, I do. I had to check this fool last week. That's why I'm down here." He hopped on my table, sat on a few leftover permission slips, and began to tell me how he landed in PSS.

"This fool got all heated 'cause I scuffed his Payless knockoff Timbos." Pacino folded his arms.

"So *did* you step on his shoes? Is that how it happened?" I asked.

"I don't know. Maybe I did. Can't remember. I just stood there and waited on him to make a move, but of course he didn't."

"So who hit who first? How did the fight jump off?"

"We just stood there — well, I stood there about to readjust his jaw, but he started to back down."

"You got in trouble for that?"

"No, man! One of my boys, Steve-O, he creeped up behind me and nudged me to the side and then threw a big bowl of chili at the dude with the fake Timbos."

"*That's* what started the fight?"

"Nope. The dude ducked and the chili hit some girl in the face. It was on then. Instant food fight."

"I heard about that food fight last week, but I didn't know who was behind it."

"Yeah, it ain't something to be proud of. He got all dirty. He had cottage cheese, beets, and that funky-smelling beef Stroganoff stuff all over his face. But me — man, I was spotless. That's why they blamed the whole thing on me," Pacino said before he looked down at his shirt to make sure he still looked fly, or at least he thought he was fly.

"So you never did fight, huh?" I asked.

"Nope. That buster better be glad them flash-light cops grabbed me. I don't let nobody, *nobody*, jump bad with me in front of the ladies." Pacino shrugged. He looked at me straight. "Who'd *you* piss off to land down here?" he wanted to know.

I didn't have a wild story like his, but I told him anyway.

"We were taking an exam in biology and this kid that sits next to me was begging to cheat off my paper. I kept ignoring him."

"So what did he do?" Pacino leaned off the edge of the table.

"Man, he kept asking for answers until crazy old Mr. Crimple saw him."

"Then you and that dude started scrappin', right?"

"Nope. Mr. Crimple thought that *both* of us were cheating! I'm not the greatest student at Locke. God knows I wish I was, but I don't cheat. It didn't matter because Mr. Crimple sent us both to Principal Richmond's office."

"When did this happen?"

"Last Friday. It was the same day your food fight popped off."

"Richmond didn't buy your good-boy routine, did he?"

I was guessing Pacino has been in Principal Richmond's office a few dozen times.

"Nope. He gave me three days of PSS this week, and gave that other kid, Tariq, three days next week. Later, Tariq snapped on me. He said that if he saw me on the streets, he was gonna stomp me until my skull collapsed."

Pacino jumped down off of the table, rolled down his sleeves, and said, "Tariq? You mean Tariq Molten?"

"That's him. You know him?" I asked.

"That's the brother I was about to knock

out in the cafeteria! Man, he ain't nothing but talk."

"He didn't seem like all talk. This *is* the same Tariq Molten that got suspended last year for breaking some kid's nose by banging it against the lockers, right?"

"Yeah, that's him. But the dude whose nose he broke was a sixth grader. A nobody. That fool Tariq had to do four months down in juvie for that. They've got a revolving door for him down there." Pacino balled up his fist, like Tariq was in the room with us.

I said to Pacino, "It wasn't my fault. He's the one that got *me* in trouble. Now he wants to step to me. People are always trying to test you, you know?"

Pacino turned and faced the clock on the wall. "That's a shame," he mumbled.

"What's a shame?" I asked.

"Tariq knows who he can put on blast and who he better not step to." Pacino shook his head.

When the giant clock on the wall hit 3:30, Mr. Patt closed his laptop. He straightened his suspenders and stood up from his desk. "Okay, get out of here. See you tomorrow. Don't be late." He waddled out of the room. Mackey was right behind him.

Before Rosilyn left, she stopped at our table, rolled her eyes at Pacino, and said to me, "See you tomorrow, boo." She blew me a kiss and then swayed her skinny frame to the door. No doubt she was cute, but I was too busy thinking about Tariq's threat.

I told Pacino, "I was going to walk home, but I kind of like my head, you know? Didn't plan on having it collapsed during this lifetime."

I checked my pockets, praying to find some spare change to ride the Metro.

"Man, don't tell me you're scared of that munchkin," Pacino joked. "I know he's fifteen and in the eighth grade, but you're a giant compared to him. I think he's one of those dudes with stunted growth or something. He should be taller than what he is. What are you goin' to do?"

"I don't know, I just don't want any problems. I don't have any beef with Tariq." I was hoping Pacino would help me out.

"Look, man, I got your back. I was goin' to smack the taste out of Tariq's mouth last week. He don't want no part of me!" Pacino fumbled for his iPod. "I'll come with you after school. You know, make sure he don't trip with you," he offered. "But first, you gotta come with me." He put his backpack over one shoulder and stood at the door, waiting for my answer.

"I mean, I'm not scared or anything. But if you want to help a brotha out and have my back just for this week, that's cool," I answered.

"Just for this week only," Pacino agreed. "I don't like Tariq, but it ain't like me and you are 'boys' or anything. Since we're gonna be hangin' out down here through Thursday, I'll do you a good deed."

I didn't really know what to say. Thanking Pacino would've made me really look like a sissy punk. I still didn't know where we were headed, so all I said was, "Where we going?"

"Just come with me. I gotta do something I do every day. Your mommy and daddy won't miss you."

We were the last ones to walk out of the PSS room and Locke Middle for the day. The afternoon seemed so quiet and still that it kind of felt like we were the first ones to see it.

3:49 P.M.
MISS LULA'S
EAST 68TH AND CLEVELAND AVENUE

I'd never been on foot headed south of the school before. I didn't have a reason to. We walked straight down Cleveland Avenue, where there's a dip as steep as the Mamba ride at Worlds of Fun. This September afternoon was disguised as late June. I folded my jacket and slid it into my backpack. Pacino just broke out laughing after we crossed East 67th Street.

"What's so funny?" I asked.

"Man, look at you. I know what I'm gonna call you — Crease." Pacino chuckled as he pulled up his sagging jeans.

"Why Crease?"

"Look at your khakis, brotha. What are those, Dockers? You must have an industrial pressing machine at the crib. And that shirt looks like

23

you showered it in starch." He kept going on about the way I dressed, how neat I was, and how "locked down" every detail about my clothes was. "Your belt is all shiny and, well, tight. Your pops must be a military man." Pacino stopped walking, faced me, and threw up a left-handed salute.

"Look, if you had my dad, you'd know how important it was to leave the house looking *presentable*. He's big on that type of thing," I explained.

"Presentable for who? A J. C. Penney catalog photographer?" Pacino wouldn't stop cracking on my clothes.

"My dad tells me and my little brother that when a man leaves the house, he's representing himself, his last name, and his family." I asked Pacino, "Doesn't your old man teach you that stuff?"

He didn't answer but kept walking. We turned left on East 68th Street. I still had no idea where we were headed. We just kept walking.

When we crossed Myrtle Avenue, Pacino turned to me and asked, "What part of Lee's Summit do you live in? Or maybe you got one of those old expensive cribs in Brookside."

"If I lived in Lee's Summit or Brookside, don't you think I'd go to school closer to where they are?"

"I don't know. You look so out of place, dog. You look geeked out right now, like you think somebody gonna jack you or something," Pacino cracked as we came up on about eight dudes playing basketball in the middle of the street. The hoop was made out of a milk crate nailed onto a light pole.

"We used to live downtown, but last year we moved to that new Citadel division off of 63rd Street."

"I knew it. A nice chunk of the suburbs slammed right down in the middle of the hood. It's gated, and it's guarded by the boys in blue, who're like shepherds watching over the good little Negro sheep." Pacino couldn't stop harping on how "creased" he thought I was.

"Citadel's cool. And I don't live that far from Alain Locke. Where do you live?"

"We passed it a few blocks ago. We live up in Meyer Heights, across the street from the school. We've been there for a minute — 'bout ten years. There's gunplay and all, but it's home to me."

"Yeah, I know about Meyer Heights," I said.

We kept walking. I didn't say anything. But him being from Meyer Heights explained a lot. It seemed like every other day after school, the police, an ambulance, or the fire department was over there. And at least once a month, Meyer Heights was on the news, adding to the homicide total in the city. Pacino and I only live ten minutes away from each other. Strange how people could live so close but not have anything in common.

When we stepped onto Jackson Avenue, I saw a yellow DEAD END sign. At the end of the block was a decrepit house. There were old bikes, a swing set, and new toys by the side of the house. In the driveway was a brand-new minivan with Jedi-black tinted windows and twenty-two-inch custom rims. There were kick balls floating in a puddle next to the curb and a homemade wooden sign with poorly painted words stuck into the ground that read:

Welcome to
MISS LULA'S HEAVENLY DAY CARE
They're all angels when they
pass through my door.
6am–6pm M–F

I didn't know what kind of circles Pacino rolled in. And now we were at some heavenly day care.

"Why are we here? One of your boys sells dope out the back and uses the day care as a front?" I tried to sting Pacino for messing with me all afternoon.

Pacino barked at me. "What? Man, shut up! That's why Tariq Molten is after you now. Just follow me and keep your mouth closed when we get up in here." The front porch was completely shaded by droopy bushes.

Pacino pushed the doorbell three times and opened the screen door. He banged his knuckles against the center of the door. I didn't know what to expect, especially when a sweet and completely harmless-looking lady opened the door and released the welcoming scent of baby powder and freshly baked oatmeal-raisin cookies. She blessed us with a warm, wide smile. Pacino immediately removed his Royals cap, then made a quick transformation into someone I hadn't seen all day.

"How's it goin', Miss Lula?" Pacino was crushing his cap with both hands like he'd just stepped into church and was trying to squash a sin.

Miss Lula spoke in a Southern hush. "Fine, just fine, Pacino. I see you've got one of your buddies with you. How you doin', baby?" Miss Lula asked me softly.

"Doing fine, ma'am." I could feel myself getting bashful. "Those cookies smell like my mom's," I said. Pacino looked over to me like he wanted to punch me in the ear.

"You kids can take some cookies with you," Miss Lula offered. "What's your name, baby?" she asked before she turned to redirect three or four small children back into their play area.

"My name is Robeson Battlefield, ma'am. I attend school with Pacino."

"Battlefield? You some kin to Reverend Battlefield over at Mount Olive? Where are your folks from?"

"My mother is from St. Louis. My dad is from Corinth, Mississippi. I don't think we're related to Reverend Battlefield. My dad would know, though."

"You kind of favor the reverend 'round the mouth and nose. That's why I'm asking. You boys have a seat." Miss Lula gestured toward her couch, which was smothered completely by plastic and needlepoint creations. Pacino grabbed me by the elbow before I could sit down.

"Not trying to be rude or anything, Miss Lula, but Robeson and I have some school stuff to do. Are the girls ready to go?" Pacino asked, still in church-boy-polite mode.

Before I could ask what girls he was talking about, Miss Lula called out toward the back of the house, "Lavi! Indi! Come on, girls! Your brother is here to get you!"

With their matching purple jackets and teddy bear backpacks, identical twins with long bouncy curls and electric laughs came running toward Pacino. They both leaped into his arms like they hadn't seen him in months. They looked to be four or five years old.

"I didn't know you had baby sisters, man," I said to Pacino.

"There's a lot you don't know, Crease. Their school bus drops them off over here after school. Anything else you need to know?" Pacino tied the shoes of one of the twins.

"Yeah. How do you tell them apart? It's probably easy for you, since they're your little sisters, right?" I asked.

"Well, Lavender, this one right here, she

laughs all the time, even when there's nothing funny. She's crazy." Pacino nudged his hands underneath Lavender's armpits, picked her up from the floor, and tickled her until her curls jiggled. "Indigo, she's a little more serious. She laughs, too, but she always wants to know the when, who, and what about stuff. That's how I tell 'em apart."

Sure enough, as soon as Pacino put Lavender down, he began to answer a bunch of kid questions from Indigo that were flung at ninety miles an hour.

"What are we having for dinner, Po?"

"Who is your friend, Po?"

"Wanna see what I did at school today, Po?"

"Is Mama gonna be at home, Po?"

Pacino answered each one as well as he could. The church boy he'd turned into for Miss Lula was now some dude from *Sesame Street*. He laughed and played with Lavender and Indigo, and made sure they had everything in their backpacks.

Pacino told his sisters, "This is Robeson, but y'all can call him Crease, okay?" They looked at me with sparkling brown eyes and silly grins. "He's just hangin' out with me today. That's all. Y'all ready?"

They both screamed, "Yeeeeees!"

Miss Lula snuck off and made us four bags filled with her oatmeal-raisin cookies and bottles of 2% milk.

"Take these, boys. Have a good evening, and y'all be safe walking home." Miss Lula showed us to the door.

"Thank you, Miss Lula." Pacino was smiling big. "My mama said she'll have the check ready for you tomorrow."

"Tell her don't worry 'bout it, baby. She can give it to me next week." Miss Lula answered with a ton of understanding in her warm voice. She gave us all a hug good-bye.

I grabbed her hand and bowed to her like she was a queen. Then I told her, "Thank you so very much for the cookies and the hospitality, Miss Lula. Really."

"Pacino, you can bring this one back anytime. A young man as respectful and nice as you are is always welcome." Miss Lula's flattery sure was sweet.

Pacino grinned at Miss Lula. But as soon as she shut the door, his smile turned off.

"What's up with you, man? I shouldn't have brought you over here. You trying to embarrass me with all of that polite charm crap?"

"Chill, Pacino. I can't help it. Polite charm is how my mama raised me." I laughed and jabbed Pacino in the arm. His expression said *Don't do that again*. "Looks like someone taught you the same thing, *Po*," I teased.

Pacino held the girls' hands as they went down the steps of Miss Lula's building. Then he turned around to me and smiled. "Good one, Crease. Good one. After I take my sisters home, I'm gonna drop you off at Tariq Molten's crib. Ha!"

When we got halfway up the block, Indigo looked up and asked Pacino the only question he didn't answer earlier. "Po, you didn't tell me so. Is Mama gonna be at home waitin' on us? Is she?"

Pacino still didn't answer. He looked down, smiled, and kept walking.

She never asked again.

Pacino told Lavender, "Girl, you know what eight plus two is. Stop foolin' around." He sat in front of the twins at their family's tiny round dining room table. He held up addition and subtraction flash cards. The twins answered everything Pacino threw their way.

"I know, I know. I was just being funny with you," Lavender giggled. Indigo looked at her with a straight face and took a long sip from her juice box. "It's ten," Lavender said. "And you know what else? Ten minus two is eight!"

Indigo gulped the last bit of juice, then jumped in. "And ten minus eight is two. I know that 'cause they all work together. Right, Po?"

"That's right, Indi! Give me some dap, baby girl," Pacino said, pumped up by their answering the right way. He held out his fists and the girls gave him some dap. It was a special double fist bump high five that could have only been created by five-year-old twin girls.

Then the twins got up and squeezed their way from around the table. They picked a book from a bookcase in the hallway. "Can we go out on the stoop and read, Po? Pleeeeeease?"

"I don't think so. You know what time it is," he said, and then pointed to their room. "Dinner's gonna be ready in a minute," he announced. They raced by us, grumbling like two little angry trolls.

Pacino's big-brother tutoring skills were better than mine. "'The purpose of education is to create in a person the ability to look at the world for himself, to make his own decisions.'" I put a hand on Pacino's shoulder. I couldn't help speechifying.

"Don't touch me, man. What are you sayin'?" He shook me off like I was the flu.

"That's Baldwin. James Baldwin. My dad has that quote on a paperweight in his office at home."

"So you just go around spouting out other dudes' stuff?" Pacino asked.

"You know James Baldwin, right?" I asked. He looked at me like I was crazy.

"Man, just because I live over here in the Heights don't mean I'm stupid. I just don't make it a point to memorize the words of dead writers. I've got real-life stuff to deal with, like these twins."

"I hear you," I said. Truth is, I help my little brother with his homework, but only sometimes. Pacino's responsibilities were quadruple mine. I followed him into the kitchen as he made the girls bowls of oxtail stew that his mother had cooked before she left for work.

"You want some? Ever had hot-water corn bread? I know you're probably used to that stuff that comes from a box."

I was quick to answer. "Hey, my dad is from Mississippi. I *know* what hot-water corn bread is." I was born in Kansas City, but my family and I spend a lot of time down south during the summer. My "country boy" comes out every now and then. I'm not new to soul food. Pacino handed me a bowl and filled it to the rim. He prepared the TV trays and we all sat in the living room in front of the twenty-seven-inch flat-screen.

The girls wanted to watch Cartoon Network. Pacino wanted to watch *106 & Park*. The twins won. Before the TV was turned on, Pacino reminded the girls to bow their heads.

"Mama ain't here, but y'all know how we do. We gotta say grace," Pacino told the twins. They held each other's hand, closed their eyes, and bowed their little heads. So did I. Pacino prayed:

"God, thank you.

"Thank you for this delicious meal that our mama has fixed for us. And thank you for Mama. She works so hard and does a great job keeping this roof over our heads, clothes on our backs, the whole nine.

"Thanks for my sisters and, of course, our extra-special guest, the good brotha Crease.

"Amen."

We all said amen and laughed. Lavender, as usual, was cracking up the most. Indigo brought us all jelly jars filled with Sunny Delight. For dessert, Pacino went into the kitchen and brought back a bag full of LaMar's famous chocolate-covered cinnamon rolls.

After dinner, the girls asked Pacino if they could go to their room and play with their toys and watch a movie. He went in to hook up the DVD player. While he was helping the girls, I checked out the many pictures that plastered every wall in the living room. The frames were so close together, they looked like puzzle pieces. They were all family pictures — new ones, old ones, black-and-whites of other family members. Smiling faces connected with me from every point of the room.

Pacino's mom must have left the radio on in her bedroom; it blared out a bunch of static from the local AM gospel station. Pacino never went in to turn it down.

He just pulled her door a little closed. No matter where I stood in that place, there was a choir belting out blessings from the bottom of their souls, and preachers praying for salvation. It seemed like God's energy floated in the apartment like the Southern aroma of that delicious oxtail stew.

In the corner behind the TV were trophies, plaques, and certificates. All school stuff. There were a few that belonged to the twins, but most of them belonged to Pacino. I saw honor roll letters, perfect 4.0 grade cards, and ribbons from academic competitions. If there was any award given away at our school for good grades, it was in this corner.

I picked up the biggest trophy that was engraved with Pacino's name. It was for a spelling bee. I was still holding the trophy when Pacino came over to where I was. "See, I knew you were the feds. Man, give me my trophy!" Pacino snarled, and then snatched the trophy from my hands.

"What are you talking about? If I had even half this stuff, I'd be a star at my house. Look at all of these awards, man. I barely make straight Bs, man." I went on about how cool it was that he kicked butt at school.

"Don't get it twisted, Crease. I ain't no punk or nothing. I just do these things to make my moms happy. That's all," Pacino explained as he carefully put his spelling bee trophy back in place.

"Nobody called you a punk because you make good grades. I wish I could do it more often. That's why we're at school, right?"

"Yeah. I guess so. But you know what I mean. Look, if you tell anybody, I'll put a lump on yo head the size of a camel hump!" Pacino threatened.

"Man, you're crazy! I wish I had your problem." I shook my head.

"I don't want other kids thinking I'm tryin' to be white or talkin' white like you do or calling me soft. You know?"

"No, I *don't* know. And who says white kids have a monopoly on being good students?" Pacino didn't answer. He just stood there facing his awards and trophies, not talking. "And I didn't know that using the English language like it's supposed to be used was a crime. *Talkin' white*...you don't know how stupid that sounds."

"Yeah. Whatever. I got a rep at that school. You don't. The only person I care about pleasing is my mama."

"Your mother looks so proud of you in that picture. What does she do for a living?" I asked.

"It depends on what day of the week. On her day shift, she's an aide at a nursing home. In the evenings, but only on Tuesdays, Thursdays, and Sundays, she works at the Target off of Wornall Road."

"Your mother works hard, huh?"

"You know it. That's why I gotta hold it down

around here. I got a little hustle on the side, too. I just feel like I'm old enough to be bringin' in some money. You know?"

"What hustle?" I asked, then I realized I didn't really want to know. "Never mind. Besides, where is your dad? And who is that tall dude in some of these family pictures on the wall? Is that your brother?" I ran off a slew of questions just like Indigo would.

Pacino snatched one of his smaller trophies, the one closest to the TV. He held it tight and sat down on the couch, which also doubled as his bed.

"As far as my dad goes, I've never seen him. Don't really think about that too much. If you see him, tell him to holla at me," Pacino joked. "But that dude right there" — he turned around and pointed at a picture of the tall kid I asked him about — "that's my big brother, Micah; he's twenty-two. That's my boy right there." Pacino stared at the picture, and then his shoulders collapsed.

"Is he . . . I mean, is he . . . gone?" I didn't know how to ask if he was dead.

"Nope, he's still here. It's almost like he's dead, though. He's up in Leavenworth serving a five-year sentence for possession. He's in his third year now." Pacino sulked.

I tossed out more questions. "Possession of what? Crack? Weed?"

"It was possession of jelly beans and licorice, dummy." He was getting sick of my Indigo impression. "Yeah, it was crack. What else?"

"Man, I don't know a lot about that stuff."

"I know you don't. Your parents got you sheltered."

"So I'm sheltered because I don't know a lot about drugs and jail time? Why are you so sarcastic?"

"I'm just talkin', Crease. Look at you gettin' all huffy," Pacino said. He popped me in my chest. "Wanna play some Xbox 360? I got that new *Halo*." Pacino pulled out what looked like an army game from beneath the coffee table.

I didn't know anything about *Halo*. My dad won't let me or my little brother, Carmichael, play video games because of the violence. Dad won't even let us *own* a game system. Seems Pacino could do whatever he wanted, though. He made the grades, and there was no one at his house most of the time to tell him no.

"I don't think I have time to play. Let me call my dad. It's almost time for guitar practice." As soon as I mentioned guitar, I wish I hadn't. I was giving Pacino ammunition.

"The *guitar*?" He laughed so hard, it looked like it hurt. "Man, who do you think you are, one of them hard-rockin' white boys?"

"My dad supports my music, but he thinks it's just a fad. He doesn't think I'm really committed to being good."

"So what does he want you to be, a civil rights leader or something?" Pacino shook his head. He wrapped the cords around the joysticks and put the game back under the coffee table.

"Dad always wants me to volunteer with him on the weekends and stuff. He even signed me up to join a speech-and-debate team at our church. I just want to do my own thing sometimes," I explained.

"That is too funny. It's okay, Crease. If you wanna be a rock star, don't let me stop you. You've got your own dreams to see out." Pacino went into his mother's room to get the cordless phone.

I called Dad, and he said he'd be right over. In the short time it took for Dad to make it, Pacino ironed the twins' clothes for school the next day, washed the dishes, and vacuumed the whole apartment.

When Dad pulled up outside of Pacino's apartment building, he honked the horn to let me know he'd arrived. The window was up in the living room. I'd know Dad's three-toot honk anywhere. At the same time, there was banging at Pacino's apartment door. Pacino put the vacuum away in the hall closet, then grabbed a small leather bag from the top shelf.

"Po! Open up, man!" a deep voice yelled outside the door.

Then another voice joined in. "Yeah, Po, we're even early. Hook us up, man!"

Pacino flipped all three of the dead-bolt locks and opened the door. There were two big kids waiting. They were at least seventeen. Both of them gave me the "what's up?" nod.

Pacino snapped at the boys, who were a lot bigger than both of us. "Hey, y'all? My sisters are about to get ready for bed. Be quiet."

"All right, li'l man. Where do you want us? The usual spot?" The biggest kid removed his Chiefs skully.

"Yeah, in the bathroom." Pacino stepped to

the side to let them in. I didn't know what was going on, but I decided to leave without getting deeper into his business.

When I was in the hallway outside the apartment, Pacino leaned out of the door and said, "Hey, Crease, remember when I said I have a side hustle?"

"Yeah . . ."

He reached in his little leather bag and pulled out two sets of barber clippers. "I know you wondered who hooked me up with this tight fade. It was me. Nobody cuts better than I do. Ten bucks a head. I'll hook your little baby 'fro up this weekend — for free! I'll get at you tomorrow, Crease." Pacino gave me a fist pound.

"Yeah, that'll be cool. See you tomorrow, man." As I walked past doors in Pacino's building, I heard wall-rattling music, a woman sobbing, gunshots and sirens from loud TVs, a baby screaming, and couples fighting.

When I walked down the steps and out of building number seven, I was a little confused. After everything that had happened that day, I honestly had no idea who the real Pacino Clapton was.

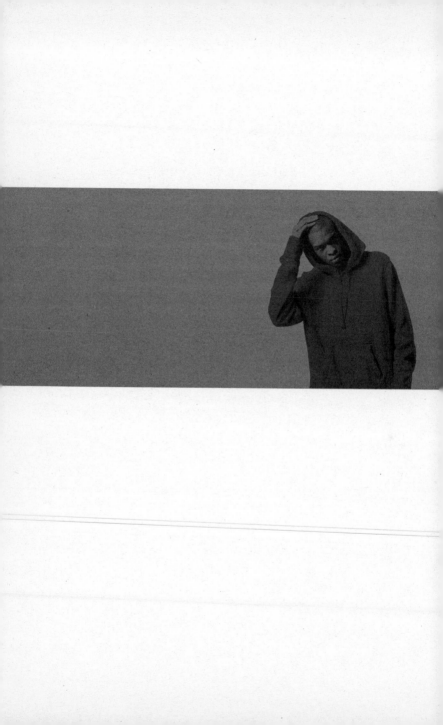

COOL
ON
WEDNESDAY

Tariq Molten was posted up with two of his boys outside of the Court. The Court is what we call our cafeteria because it's built like a basketball arena. Down in the center, where the game would be, is where we get our food.

Third period had just ended, and I went to my locker on the first floor, the same floor the Court is on. Usually, I'm with my boy Nazr, but he was out sick. Truth is, Nazr wasn't really *sick*, but that's what he told his mom. The real story is that Nazr's cousin from Indianapolis was in town, and she and Nazr went to a Royals game. The Royals had the Yankees in a three-game home stand. I didn't blame Nazr for being sick. When I saw Tariq and his boys, I wished I could have been "sick," too. And I would have loved to zap myself into Kauffman Stadium, far away from the Court.

Tariq and his boys were tripping kids they didn't know and slapping girls on the butt for fun. Maybe I could cut down the side hallway and slip to the Court from the other side. When the classes from the second floor let out, I was sandwiched between seventh and sixth graders changing classes. But one of Tariq's boys spotted me. I was trapped.

He was a cocky kid with ragged cornrows. He leaned into Tariq, whispered something, then pointed in my direction. I couldn't sneak away. I had no choice but to keep walking between the seventh- and sixth-grade kids. Tariq looked dead at me and started nodding like he'd been looking for me.

Tariq's other boy, a lanky dude with long arms, was hyped. He turned and punched the lockers twice. Tariq and his boy switched from harassing girls to watching my every move. They looked ready to beat me down.

I'd never been in a real fight; I could always sense when something bad was about to happen. This was one of those times. Tariq made his right hand into a gun, pointed, aimed, and shot at me with four imaginary slugs.

I backed up like I didn't see them, turned around, and walked fast down the side hallway, where a stairwell leads up to the main office. When I looked back down the hallway, Tariq and one of his boys were chasing me. I kept my cool. I didn't run. I shut the door behind me and started to climb the stairs to the main office.

The door slammed behind me with an echo. When I started to climb the stairs, I looked up and into the face of Tariq's tall friend standing there. "Didn't think we saw you, huh?" He pounded a fist in his other hand and then folded his arms like he was getting ready to jack me up.

"I was heading up to the office," I told him as I started to step backward down the stairs.

"I don't think so. My boy Tariq's got something to holla at you about." He started coming toward me.

"Look who we have here." Tariq laughed when he came through the door at the bottom of the stairwell. His other boy, the one with the corn-rows, was right behind him. I was trapped for sure. Where was Pacino when I needed him?

I turned to Tariq. "Hey, . . . what's up, man?" It's hard to fake a smile when you're not feeling it.

"What's up is that you're about to be the lead story on the five o'clock news." Tariq was wearing a black hoodie. Both of his hands were deep in his front pockets. "Lean up against that door, Chauncey," he ordered the cocky corn-row dude.

"This is the little dude you were talking about?" asked Chauncey. "You can definitely handle this one yourself, T." He leaned against the door like Tariq told him to.

"What's the problem? Is this about the test?" I set my book bag on the floor between us. "*You're* the one that got us in trouble." I said with a little bit of irritation in my voice.

The tall kid came marching down the steps. He stood in my face like he wanted to chin-check me. "He sounds like he got a beef with *you*, Tariq. How you gonna handle this? What you want me to do?"

Tariq held his hand up. "It's cool, Poke. I got this one. If you woulda just gave me the answer, fool, neither one of us would be in PSS."

"Why should I have given you the answers? If you didn't study, that's on you." I figured they were going to jump me anyway, so I said my piece loud and solid.

Poke and Chauncey made the situation worse. "Daaaaaaang!"

Poke pumped up Tariq. "You gonna let him just jump bad with you like that, T? Handle yo business, boy. Handle yo business!"

"Look at you. I can see the fear all over your face." Tariq was right up on me. But his hands were still in his pockets. I didn't know what he was about to do. Maybe I had said too much. He said, "I don't like punks with big mouths."

"Man, why are you messing with me over a test?" I asked.

"Being put in PSS got me in trouble with my PO. One more thing and I'll probably have to —" Tariq stopped himself mid-sentence, then shoved his hands deeper into his pockets. The fact that he had a real-life parole officer was proof that he was a sneeze away from being another statistic.

Chauncey told Tariq, "Quit talking to this fool. Are you gonna do it or what?" Whatever they had planned for me, it didn't look like Tariq was ready to go through with it.

"I'm about to. I'm about to. Don't rush me!" My insides were pounding. I thought for sure the school security guard, Mr. Thompson, would have kicked in the door by then. But there wasn't even a knock. Not one soul came down the stairs to break up the mess that was about to happen.

Tariq started fumbling with something in his right pocket, but he couldn't pull it out. His boys were getting jumpy. "Hurry up! Pop him!" Poke shouted.

But before any popping went off, I heard Mr. Thompson at the top of the stairs. "Who's down there? You need to be at lunch or in a classroom! Get out of here!"

"I'm gone!" Chauncey was the first to break.

Poke raced down the stairs past me. On his way out of the stairwell, he bumped me hard with his shoulder, knocked me down.

I was on the floor, looking up at Tariq. He hocked a loogie and spit down on me like I was nothing. He missed my head, but a big glob of slobber splattered close to my face. "Next time, they gonna be calling yo folks to come get you from the hospital," he said before he flew out the door.

Mr. Thompson made it to the bottom of the stairs and helped me to my feet. "You all right? What are you doing here?"

"I was just . . . I was headed to the office. But I slipped and fell," I lied.

"Get to lunch or class or wherever you're supposed to be. I've got more important things to do. Go — now!"

I didn't say anything. I just nodded yes. I was glad Mr. Thompson showed up, but not for my sake, for Tariq's. He had no idea what I was capable of.

2:51 P.M.
ALAIN LOCKE MIDDLE SCHOOL
THE POST-SCHOOL SUSPENSION ROOM

"Maaaaaan, you are crazy! Wayne is the best MC on the planet. You must be smokin', boy," Pacino went off while we compared our favorite rappers.

"If a rapper has *lil'*, *young*, or *yung* before his name, he sucks. I'm sorry, that's just the way it is." I was defending Common, my favorite MC.

It was twenty minutes into PSS, and neither one of us had even started on assigned work. We didn't care, and neither did Mr. Patt. He was in the semifinals of an online sudoku tournament. Mackey had his head down at his station. Rosilyn was the only one paying attention. She was deep into our conversation. But I could tell by her nods, the way she threw her head back, and her laughs that she was on Pacino's side. Rosilyn was feeling Wayne.

I had my arms folded b-boy style. "Man, you don't know what real hip-hop is, do you? I'm talking about that old-school stuff." Rosilyn covered her mouth and was cracking up. "Ever heard of Big Daddy Kane? EPMD? Eric B. & Rakim? I didn't think so." This made her laugh even more.

"I ain't never heard of them lames you just named," Pacino smirked. "If they don't get any play on the radio, on TV, or in the club, they don't matter anymore. Weezy *is* hip-hop. *He's* getting airtime, not those jokers you mentioned."

"That radio garbage ain't hip-hop," I told him. "My dad has all of his old hip-hop tapes and CDs. I know what's up."

"What does your *pops* know about hip-hop?" Pacino asked.

"Enough. He's a music professor at U of Missouri KC. He teaches a music history course that's about appreciating all types of music. Plus, he ain't that old, man. The rappers he listened to talked about real stuff."

"Real stuff like what? If I want to hear some preachin', I'll go to church. It's always been about bangin' beats." Pacino stood up and started to count down on his left hand. Rosilyn jumped all on his team. She testified and waved her hands like one of the old ladies who have been members of the congregation for years.

"Yep. Tight beats," she agreed.

"Money . . ." Pacino continued.

"It's always about the *money*, boy," Rosilyn piggybacked.

Pacino kept it going. "The jewelry. The gear."

"Oh yeah. We stay laced in nice clothes and diamonds, baby." Rosilyn was on her feet, dancing around.

"And of course, it's gonna always be about the young ladies," Pacino bragged with his arms folded. He shot me a b-boy stance. "And my nig—" He stopped himself before saying the whole *N* word.

I shook my head. "See, there you go again. That's why I don't listen to a lot of that radio crap. The words that they use to describe us just ain't cool, especially the *N* word."

Rosilyn and Pacino looked at each other, then said at the same time, "What *N* word? Nig—?"

"Yeah, yeah, yeah." I stopped them before they could use that word on me. "That's the one. Calling each other the *N* word just ain't cool."

"Says who?" Rosilyn laughed and then gave Pacino some dap. They were both cracking up, but I was serious.

"It's just not a word I grew up hearing my dad use around my house," I explained. "Y'all just throw it around like it's no big deal."

Rosilyn put a hand on my shoulder and popped her gum. "It ain't a big deal, Robeson. You know your name. If I call you 'my nig,' that's something good, boo." She winked at me and smiled through lips caked with sparkly gloss.

"It's *not* a good thing, Rosilyn. I hate to hear that word and I don't like it when somebody says it to me. It's not something I want to be called." She shook her head like she was trying to understand where I was coming from.

"Crease, you're crazy. What should I say if I see you in the hallway?" The b-boy smirk had not left Pacino's face. "I know," he said, "how about brother?" He held out his fist to give me a pound. "What's good, *brotha*?"

I pounded him back even though I knew he was playing. "Brother sounds a lot better."

Pacino looked at me like he couldn't care less. "Whatever, *brotha*. That just ain't the way I get down. But if you want me to call you brotha,

I will. Nobody will believe we're really brothas anyway."

"Why's that, Pacino?" Rosilyn asked.

"Look at how ugly Crease is. Besides, I'm the finest nig — I mean, *brotha*, at this school."

We all laughed.

Mr. Patt was still locked on sudoku. He pumped his fist and yelled out, "Got 'em! I'm headed to the finals, baby!" We could have walked out of PSS and he wouldn't have noticed.

"I understand you, Robeson." Rosilyn grinned. "And I think you look pretty good. You aiight, boo. Plus your daddy sounds like a good man. You talk about him every day."

Pacino jumped in. "Don't he? Can't you think for yourself, boy?"

"My father teaches me a lot of stuff. Nothing wrong with that," I said.

"I'm just frontin'," Pacino said. "Your pops sounds cool. Matter of fact, I wanna meet him, 'cause I feel like I already know him."

"You're serious?" I asked. "I mean . . . he might pick me up tomorrow." At first I thought Pacino was just joking, but something sad in his eyes told me he wasn't.

"How about today, Crease? I had you all up in my spot yesterday, around my baby sisters, and even gave yo sorry butt some of my mama's oxtail stew. Today it's your turn, brotha!" Pacino had invited himself over before I'd even thought about it. He did have a point. How could I say no?

"Sure, yeah, I guess so," I said. "What about your sisters? Don't you have to pick them up today?"

"Nope. My mama is off this evening. I wanna see how the good side lives. I gotta meet the famous Battlefield clan. Y'all probably live like a TV family or something."

"TV family? Come on, man. We're just regular folks. My mother is cool. My little brother is cool. My father, my sister in college — we're all just regular."

Pacino balled up an old piece of paper and threw it at me. Rosilyn caught the ball before it hit me in my face. "Yeah, okay. Whatever, Crease," Pacino said.

Rosilyn leaned closer to me, smelling like sweet-pink bubble gum and hair gel. "I got you, Robeson. If he can come over today to meet your daddy and stuff, how about you have me over tomorrow to meet yo mama?" she whispered.

Rosilyn was inches away from plastering my cheeks with her sparkly lip gloss. I knew it was coming. I did.

"I knew it, I knew it!" Pacino shouted. "I knew you liked her, Crease."

And I sure couldn't figure out what to expect by bringing Pacino Clapton to my house.

3:42 P.M.
THE METRO
63RD STREET WEST ROUTE

"Dummy, you know we can't use those anymore." Pacino laughed at me as he snatched the two bus transfers I had in my hand. He balled the transfers, then threw them in my face. "These were from two weeks ago. Transfers expire in hours." I never really ride the Metro. My dad picks me up and drops me off.

"I don't have any change on me. Do you?" I looked over Pacino's shoulder and saw the 63rd Street westbound coming fast from three blocks away.

"Do *I* have any money? You know I keep some paper on me, boy." Pacino pulled out a stack of tens, fives, and a few twenties. He handed me five ones like it was nothing and then started to sing in a high-pitched voice: *"I'm a hustla, baby!"*

"All of that is haircut money?" I asked.

"Haircut-hustle money. The light bill ain't gonna pay itself." Pacino folded his money like it was a napkin, then slid it back into his pocket.

"You pay your family's electric bill?"

"Yeah, sometimes. Whatever my mama needs, I try to make it happen, you know?"

I nodded, but I didn't really know what it was like to pay bills for a family. I got an allowance for doing stuff around the house, but that money was mine to keep.

The bus came to a whistling stop. The bus driver looked tired. Her dreary eyes were focused straight ahead. She blinked a few times, then adjusted her seat belt. There was an old lady sitting in the front with purple-gray hair, and an even older man in a wheelchair sitting close to the door near the back.

Pacino got on before I did, put money in the fare box, then went way to the back. I paid and sat somewhere in the middle of the bus, just a few rows ahead of Pacino.

"Crease! Why you up there, square?" Pacino yelled out. He leaned against his window, plugged in his iPod, and stared out.

I got up from my seat and walked back to sit with Pacino.

"So what do you know about Tariq Molten?"

Pacino must have had the volume on his iPod low, because he answered. "Why? Why do you care?"

"I don't know. Just asking." I didn't want to tell him about Tariq and his boys almost jumping me on the stairs. He already thought I was a chump.

Pacino tugged his earbuds out. "Tariq's mama's an alcoholic. He's had about ten stepdaddies, and I hear that almost all of them whupped his butt on the daily. He used to come to school with busted lips and black eyes." When we hit a red light, Pacino stared out the window on his side of the bus. "Tariq ran away from home about three years ago, and goes in and out of different group homes."

"Doesn't he have other family members?"

"Yeah, I guess so. Every now and then, his grandma will come get him, I hear. But then he'll do something stupid again and end up right back in trouble. I think even his granny has given up on him."

"Man, I didn't know all that."

"Come on now, Crease." Pacino shrugged.

"What? All I said was Tariq's got it bad."

"He's got it bad? Everybody's got it bad but you. Now you feeling sorry for this fool?" Pacino put his earbuds back in and turned his head away from me. I went back to my old seat farther up.

The closer we got to our stop, the better things looked out the bus windows. In my subdivision, the Citadel, houses were big, roofs were wide and new, and lawns were as green as the turf out at Arrowhead Stadium. Pacino picked up on it right away.

"Mansions in the hood," he said. "And what's so cool is, one of them belongs to you!" Pacino cheered. "Like I said, you got it good, Crease."

"I just live here," I said. "My dad reminds us that nothing we have came free. God can take it away just like that."

"Whatever, Crease. I don't know which one of those joints you live in, but if it was me, I'd throw a party up in that piece every weekend, with all my boys and music, and *ladies* everywhere."

"Citadel!" announced the bus driver. I grabbed my stuff and stepped off the bus at the front. I thought Pacino was behind me, but he'd already slipped out the bus's back door. He was helping the bus driver lower the elderly man in the wheelchair onto the sidewalk.

"How's that? You cool?" Pacino asked the man as he rolled him over to the sidewalk.

"That'll do just fine. Thank you, young brotha." The man was all smiles.

We watched him nudge the little lever that controlled his motorized wheelchair and cross the street toward Harold Pener Men's Wear. "Pacino, man, that was cool."

"Crease, that ain't nothing new for me. I'm always willing to help my fellow *brotha*, even an *old* brotha. You haven't figured me out yet?"

I gave Pacino the brother-to-brother up-nod. Together we walked down the hill that leads to my house.

One of the three garage doors was wide open. My mom's new Infiniti was inside; Dad's Touareg was parked in front of the middle door. I knew the third slot in the garage was empty. My sister usually parks there when she comes home over her breaks from college.

"This is *sweet*, Crease. You got a good life, and I haven't even seen the whole house yet." Pacino dropped his bag on the floor and looked around like he was in the Taj Mahal. "There's gotta be at least three bedrooms, right? Four?"

"Five."

"Five bedrooms? This is a hotel, man. I gotta see your room. You probably have a two-lane bowling alley up there."

"Man, just come in." I triggered the sensor to close the garage door.

When we got inside the house, we stepped into my dad's latest and biggest home-improvement project — an entertainment theater that Dad and a couple of his construction friends finished a couple of weeks ago. The carpet is plush, and the brown leather love seats make us feel like we're at a big Hollywood private viewing for a new film. The best part, other than the sur-round sound, is the ninety-five-inch projector screen and framed movie posters.

Pacino was all eyes. "I knew Battlefield sounded like a name for rich folks. Your parents are paid."

"Look, it's no big deal."

Pacino was all over it. "I'll be coming to watch all of the Chiefs games for the rest of the season in this no-big-deal."

There was a stack of big boxes from the enter-tainment equipment that formed an aisle lead-ing to the love seats. Carmichael, my little brother, jumped from behind one of the boxes, wearing his Darth Vader mask and holding a toy lightsaber. He let out what was supposed to be a scary "GRRRRRRRRRRR!!!"

Pacino jumped back.

"Pacino, this is my little brother, Carmichael. He's eight."

"I'm almost nine!"

"So what. You're eight now," I said. I flipped his mask up on his forehead and untangled his cape.

Pacino was laughing. "Carmichael, huh? How about I just call you Money Mike?" Pacino had his hand out, waiting for my little brother to give him some dap. Carmichael left him hanging.

"I would shake your hand . . . but I don't think so." Carmichael pulled his mask back down over his face, held his lightsaber up, and posed like a Jedi knight.

"Man," Pacino said. "I can't believe I just got dissed by an eight-year-old. What's up with your little brother, Crease?"

"You gotta excuse him," I apologized. "He's nothing like me."

"You got that right," Carmichael said. He flipped his mask back up on his forehead, turned toward Pacino, and preached, "Hey, if we're going to be cool, you can at least respect me enough to call me by my real name."

Pacino couldn't stop laughing. "That's cool, li'l dude. Sorry 'bout that. Carmichael, right?" Pacino put out his hand again.

"Carmichael Battlefield. The one and only. Nice to meet you, brotha," he said. They finally shook hands. "Are you eating with us, Pacino?" Carmichael asked.

Pacino looked at me and shrugged. "Am I, Crease? It sure smells fine, whatever it is." The smell of my mom's cooking floated from the kitchen, down the stairs, around a corner, and danced right into our noses.

"I *think* my mom will be cool with you staying for dinner," I answered, not really sure.

Carmichael jumped in. "We always welcome guests, Robeson. You know that."

He fixed his mask and took off running with his red cape flapping. "I'll run up to ask her to set another place at the table."

"Wait a minute, Carmichael!" I called out. "What about the report you turned in Monday? Did you get it back today?"

Carmichael ran back into the room, pulled his mask off again, and said, "Sure did. . . . Got a hundred percent, Robeson. Ms. Basil loved it!"

Now I was the one giving dap to my little brother.

"Hey, Carmichael, didn't I tell you that Steve Biko would be a good choice?"

"You sure did. Thanks for the tip, Robeson. Gotta go." He took off running again.

Pacino gave me some dap, and I returned the favor. "You help your li'l brother with his school-work, too?" he asked.

"I just gave him the idea. My dad usually helps him with the nitty-gritty day-to-day home-work. I'm not the brainiac that you are, geek," I joked with Pacino.

Pacino faked a threat with his palm stiff in midair, ready to strike. "Man, I'll smack you in the back of the neck. I ain't no brainiac geek, man."

4:44 P.M.
BATTLEFIELD RESIDENCE
THE KITCHEN

The smell of my mom's lasagna pulled us up the stairs.

Pacino and I went into the kitchen like hungry lasagna zombies. "I know I'm staying now. Your mama must be a chef."

Mom was standing in front of the sink with one hand on a hip and the other holding a cordless phone. She was looking out over our backyard, talking to her friend.

"Okay . . . okay, girl. It's time for dinner . . . yeah. Robeson brought one of his friends home. . . . I'll see you at the airport tonight, Patty. Bye." Mom wiped her hands on a dish towel, turned around, and smiled at Pacino and me.

"Why are you going to the airport tonight?" I asked.

"Anybody ever told you that it's bad manners to eavesdrop?"

"Sorry. . . . So where are you going?"

"I'm going to the entrepreneurs' conference in Maryland. You forgot, old man?"

Mom is always traveling on business. I forget about her trips lots of times. She could tell by the lost look on my face that this was one of those times.

She pinched me on the cheek and then gave me a hug and kiss. She nodded to Pacino. "Who is this handsome friend of yours?" Pacino shoved his hands into his pockets. For the first time ever, he looked nervous.

"Mom, this is Pacino," I said.

"How are you doin', ma'am? I'm Pacino Clapton." He transformed again into the nice dude he was over at Miss Lula's place. Like Miss Lula, my mom eats that stuff up, but she was watching Pacino carefully, figuring out who this kid was.

"Nice to meet you. Are you an eighth grader as well?" Mom straightened out her Florida A&M T-shirt. She never misses an opportunity to proudly display the loud orange-and-green seal of her alma mater.

"Yes, ma'am, eighth."

My mom kept smiling, but she was checking out Pacino's rough clothes and hair. That's a skill Mom has. She makes you feel comfortable, but at the same time she's looking you over to see what you're about. "And I'm sure you're one of the better students at Locke. Am I right, Pacino?" Mom asked.

"You know it, Mrs. Battlefield. I hit the books hard. I keep a 3.6 GPA or above." The trophies and stuff at his house said Pacino was telling no lie.

"Excellent, Pacino," Mom said. "Robeson does his best. Right, baby? In fact, every time he brings home a good grade, we try to do something special for him to keep him motivated."

"Come on, Mom," I said. "Look, my grades are improving."

"Whatever you say, Robeson." Pacino patted me on my head like I was a stray mutt or something.

"Well, Pacino, if you can just make sure Robeson stays on the right track academically, you're welcome over here anytime for dinner," Mom said.

"Yes, ma'am."

Mom had given Pacino the once-over too many times. Even with her way of keeping it on the down-low, it was hard not to notice how sloppy this brother looked to her, with his wrinkled pants hanging low and sneakers all jacked up. Pacino never really looked at Mom straight. His eyes were always ducking hers. And he kept jerking at his pants, working hard to keep them up.

Even my work-the-charm mom didn't fully know what to say to Pacino. I could tell she was keeping it cool but not totally feeling this kid as a friend of mine.

Pacino knew it, too. He was far from home in every way. If Pacino's raggedy sneakers could have grown wings to fly him out of here, he'd have been gone. His eyes had hardly left his feet. It was like he was trying to find something he'd stashed in his socks.

Finally, Mom said, "By the time you boys come back from washing your hands, the food should be on the table. Hurry, now!"

5:03 P.M.
BATTLEFIELD RESIDENCE
THE OFFICE

I let Pacino use the bathroom first, the one across the hall from my father's office. Pacino was taking forever, and I started to do the I-have-to-pee dance.

"Man, hurry up in there!" I banged on the door.

Dad's office door was closed, but I could hear his fingers tap-dancing on his computer keyboard and soft music escaping from beneath the door.

Pacino finally came out. "What's wrong with you, Crease? Can't a *brotha* use it in peace?" He'd managed to yank his pants up a bit, and it looked like he'd wetted his face.

While I was washing my hands, I heard Dad open his office door. He introduced himself to Pacino. "Come on in, young man. You like Bach's music?"

"Is that what you're listening to . . . sir? You're into that stuff?" I heard Pacino ask.

"Music of all sorts is what I do; I'm a student of every genre of music, son," Dad said.

"This is some I could do without. Seems cold as ice."

That's when I came out of the bathroom as fast as I could. Nobody disses Dad's music.

Pacino was thumbing through a gigantic, dark brown, leather-bound hunk of pages covering the history of classical music. Dad had about a little over twenty wooden CD pedestals positioned around his office, each one showcasing a "bible" or collective history of every major music genre, even one on hip-hop.

Even though Dad and Pacino had met, I started to introduce them. "This is Pacino, Dad."

"We've already met, and I know this man can speak for himself. I've heard him." Now dad was giving Pacino the eye, checking out his clothes. Pacino was ready to defend. Before Dad could even ask, he was explaining himself.

"It's Pacino, like the actor. You know . . . Scarface?" Pacino explained, easing his way over to Dad's rock 'n' roll CD pedestal.

Dad pulled his favorite Jimi Hendrix and showed it to Pacino. He was playing it cool, but I could tell he was about to do some digging.

"Pacino, an intriguing name. Are your parents Italian?"

"No, sir, they just thought the name sounded cool," Pacino said, still thumbing through the CDs.

Pacino walked over to the jazz CD pedestal and started flipping.

Dad handed him a Miles Davis. "Take it, Pacino. There's no ice in Miles."

Pacino gave Dad an up-nod. He was slow to take the CD. "I can borrow it? For real?" He was so excited, it seemed like Dad was letting him hold on to an actual trumpet from Mr. Davis himself.

"For real," Dad said.

Right then, Carmichael stormed in. "Dinner!" he shouted.

"Let's grub," I said.

Pacino gave one swift yank to his pants. His jeans had begun to sag way down.

We turned to leave the office, but Dad stopped us. "Robeson, before you get to the dining room, get your friend a belt." Pacino looked busted. Dad said, "If you're going to dine with us, you gotta come to the table correct."

"Its okay, Mr. Battlefield. I'll just pull 'em up. I always wear my gear like this." Pacino was trying to be cool, but the pants were droopy and looked stupid.

"Not good enough, Pacino." Dad took off his glasses, hung them from his collar. "What if I wore my pants like that? Do you think my students would listen to me?"

Pacino shrugged. "I don't . . . well, . . . maybe they . . ."

"No, they wouldn't. They wouldn't respect me as a teacher or as a man." Dad was gearing up to lecture. He took his glasses out from his collar, cleaned them off with a suede rag that he keeps in his pocket, and then slid them back on his face.

"You're probably right. I don't know," Pacino mumbled.

I really felt for Pacino. Dad could get preachy. "Dad, it's okay. Really." But my pops wasn't buying it.

"Your last name is Clapton, right?"

"Yes, sir." Pacino answered like a little kid.

"That name means something to your folks, and it should mean something to you." Dad tapped Pacino on the chest twice. "No real man walks out of the house looking like a clown. You gotta know that. If for nobody else, wear the belt for *you*, Clapton."

Bam! Dad was laying it down hard.

Pacino looked like he wanted to defend his "droopy drawers," but the brother was dried up for a comeback. He nodded once, then managed to say, "You're right, Mr. Battlefield. This is your house. I respect it and you." Then he turned to me. "Come on, man, let's go get that belt. I'm starving."

"Good deal. Thanks for understanding, young brotha," Dad said to Pacino. As we turned to walk out the door, Dad landed a hand on Pacino's shoulder. "Hey, man, just because you wear a belt doesn't mean your pants need to be pulled up to your chest. You know what I'm saying?"

Dad could always lighten a blow after he'd delivered it. He'd put Pacino at ease.

Pacino laughed. "Yeah, I got it."

"You don't have to be a square, a chump, or whatever term you guys use these days. You can still look decent with a belt on."

"I guess . . . I mean yeah, okay." Pacino was out of the office fast, holding tight to his Miles Davis CD.

5:19 P.M.
BATTLEFIELD RESIDENCE
THE DINING ROOM
BLESSING THE MEAL

"It's about time!" When we got to the dining room, Carmichael was at the table, ready to grub.

Mom noticed the belt on Pacino's pants. She looked at Dad, then me. "You can sit next to Robeson, Pacino. Carmichael will sit next to me tonight."

Pacino slid onto the seat next to me. He kept shifting his seat, uneasy. Mom asked Dad to bless the food. She held Dad's hand, then mine. Pacino slid his hands in his pockets.

"Come on, man, reach," Carmichael said as he stretched across the table as much as he could to catch Pacino's hand.

Pacino was slow to take one hand out of his pocket, but he reached out to Carmichael. He took his other hand out of his pocket and grabbed my hand fast. He wouldn't look at me, but his grip was firm.

"Everything smells delicious, Celeste," Dad said, complimenting my mom's cooking skills.

Dad bowed his head and began to pray over the food, like he does every night: *"Thank you for this blessed evening. I thank you for my beautiful, loving wife, Celeste, who prepared this magnificent meal. Thank you for my children: Carmichael, Robeson, and Laila. And thank you, Lord, for the presence of our guest, Pacino Clapton. Walk with us and guide our steps."*

Pacino was the first to say *"Amen."*

After dinner I took Pacino upstairs to show him my room before he went home. Dad said that he would give Pacino a ride. "Well, . . . here it is. It's nothing special, but it's my spot; this is where the magic happens," I said.

Pacino was back to acting like he always did — giving me a hard time about my style. "What magic? Ironing your khakis? Twiddling your thumbs? Strumming your guitar? Magic. Yeah, right." He looked around, dropped his bag on the floor, and then hit me with a face full of disappointment.

There's no TV in my room, so no video games

and no DVD player, either. But everything was where it was supposed to be. The bed was made perfectly: no lumps, no bumps, and no lines. The floor was clean: no shoes, no paper, no dirty underwear, and no dust. My guitar was propped up on a stand.

"Crease, I could have had dinner up here — on the floor! Brother, you a neat freak!" Pacino laughed.

He looked around and noticed how naked my walls were. The only thing hanging up was a big poster of the Last Supper over my bed. In this one, Jesus is black, and his disciples are people like Marcus Garvey, Mary McLeod Bethune, Malcolm X, Martin Luther King, Jr., and Booker T. Washington.

"Now, that's cool. A black Jesus — I'm feeling that one."

I showed Pacino my NFL players autograph collection.

"My dad knows a couple of them, like Jamaal Charles and Tamba Hali."

Pacino stared at the collection like he was looking at a suitcase of dollar bills. "This is better than black Jesus. Why don't you get one of these big football dudes to take out Tariq

Molten for you?" He was running his finger over one of the autographs. "You never know, the next time Tariq and his boys run up on you, you might not be so lucky to get away."

"How'd you find that out?" Pacino knew that I almost got jumped earlier in the day?

"There ain't much that goes on at school that I don't know about. Anyway, kids are calling you a punk, man. Everybody."

"I don't care. The people that you're talking about, I probably don't even know them."

"You better start to care, Crease. Tariq don't play. I wish I could've been there to help," Pacino offered with a shrug. "I can't be around every waking moment."

"Meaning?" I asked.

"Meaning that Tariq will go all out. He's street. You ain't even. That's real." Pacino tried to explain to me the best way to get out of a Tariq Molten beatdown. "Don't even try to fight back. Just take his little weak punches, go down, and keep it movin'."

It was time I showed Pacino what I was really about.

"Pacino, come over here and check this out." We stepped over to my walk-in closet. I swung open both doors like we were entering a secret bank safe. On the left side hung all of my clothes.

"Your Poindexter wardrobe? That's what you wanted to show me?" Pacino asked. I didn't answer. I just turned on the closet light and exposed my biggest secret, a secret that no one at my school knew.

"Crease, what is all of this?" Pacino's face was spray-painted with shock.

"That one there, the silver one, I won last month. First place in the annual Midwestern Martial Arts Conference and Competition." The entire right side of my closet was lined with trophies ranging from statuettes to one as tall as me.

"Let me get this right — you won these? I mean, they look like karate trophies. I must be trippin'!" Pacino held a trophy in each hand. "Man, there has to be almost thirty awards here. How'd you do it, Crease?"

"It's called kyokushin and it's built on the martial arts principles of self-improvement, discipline, and hard training."

Pacino, still in awe of all of the hardware I had on display, put the two trophies down and read my name on a bigger one, a huge bowl.

"*Kyo*-what? Is that like karate?" he asked.

"It's a sparring version. I've been training and competing ever since I was six."

"Crease, man, you are a secretive dude. Have you ever knocked somebody out, broke some bones, or got chin-checked yourself?"

"That's not really what kyokushin is about. I didn't get into it to see how many people I could hurt," I answered. "It's about soundness of mind, not kicking butts."

"Dang, Crease! I would have never guessed!"

Pacino bumped his shoulder to mine. "So if you're so good, how come you need me to watch your back? Tariq Molten wouldn't step to you if he knew what kind of skills you had. You could cripple that boy."

"I've never had a *real-real* fight in my life. I compete for the sport, the competition. Tariq seems like he's for real. I know he or one of his boys probably carries a gun, or a knife, or brass knuckles or something."

"Brass knuckles? Man, what you think this is, *Grease*? *West Side Story*?" Pacino cracked up.

"What do you know about those movies?" I asked.

"You ain't the only one with a Blockbuster card." I laughed when Pacino yelled out

"Hi-yaaaa!!!" after he pulled a video rental card out of his wallet.

"Okay, well maybe not brass knuckles, but you know what I mean. I know *you* know what I mean. Dudes like Tariq and his boys, dudes like . . ." I paused.

"Go ahead, say it — thugged-out delinquents that keep a nine in their backpacks? Is that what you mean? Dudes like me, right?" Pacino asked.

"Yeah, I guess so. Tariq seems like the kind of dude that could get a gun real easy."

"Hey," Pacino said. "Why don't you show me some of those deadly, nose-busting, bone-breaking kyo-whatever moves that you know." Pacino made some fake karate moves. "You may not want to bust Tariq up, but I ain't got no problems doin' him in. You know what I mean?"

"I don't want to hurt Tariq or anyone. He's got enough problems. Ever heard of just avoiding a fight?" I asked.

"Yeah, I heard of it. And I'm not talkin' about that stuff that happened in the stairwell. I'm talkin' about a real fight. The last time I tried to 'avoid' a fight, I was left with blood on my face." Pacino pointed to the scar on his cheek. "If I were you, I'd handle Tariq before he handles you."

"You're *not* me. The martial arts are serious, plus, you need to learn something about self-control."

"Self-control? I'll control this fist upside his head and put him to sleep for good."

"There you go again, Pacino. That's what I'm saying. Everything has to come down to some-body getting hurt. My dad says prisons and graveyards are running over with brothas, young and old. And he says that we don't need to add to that population."

"There *you* go, quoting your dad again. You saw where I live. That's how you have to think or else you'll get your butt beat on the daily." Pacino laid it down seriously. "Tell me, Crease, do you have one original thought? Your pops has programmed you. You're like a puppet around that man."

Pacino could diss me, but not my dad. "A pup-pet? He's my dad, man. At least he makes sense. Let's say you hurt Tariq or keep thinking that everything has to be handled by fighting and stuff, then you'll be sharing a jail cell with your dumb brother. Is that what you want? Your mother will have two boys in the joint. You think that will make her happy?"

Pacino's jaw got tight. "See, you didn't even have to mention that." The joking, talks of karate lessons, and taking care of Tariq Molten had slammed into a stone wall. He wasn't smiling anymore. "Why'd you have to put my brother in this?"

"Because this is about brothers. It's about you and me. You can't go around thinking you're tougher than everybody else, Pacino. My dad —" I began, before Pacino cut me off.

"*Yo daddy. Yo daddy. Yo daddy.* Man, forget you and your daddy. You think you're better than me 'cause you live over here?" he spat. "You think you're better than me because your folks got a little money, and you don't have to worry about bullets flying through your bedroom walls at night, right?"

"No, man. I never said that. I was just —"

"Come on, Crease, you thought I was just the type of dude that wouldn't mind getting shot or getting into a fight for somebody. You think your life means more to you than mine does to me?"

"The way you talk sometimes, it doesn't seem like you care about anybody but yourself."

"It's like that, right?" he asked before he snatched his bag from the floor and made his way toward the door. "Let's see how you do without me. I hope they catch up with you. You think they look at you like a brother, *brotha*? I'll tell your pops that I'm ready to bounce. I'm out."

Pacino threw me the illest mean-mug ever made by a human face. He charged out of my room and never looked back.

BOYS
ON
THURSDAY

10:27 A.M.
ALAIN LOCKE MIDDLE SCHOOL
THE AUDITORIUM

"One more time, students. Let's stand up and give a *warmer* and more *enthusiastic* round of applause for Dr. McKinney and his all-star staff of award-winning, traveled archaeologists." Principal Richmond's shadow draped over the first twenty rows of the auditorium. His voice was ten-ton heavy and his suit was wide, black, and serious.

Even though all of us were bored out of our domes, we stood up and clapped a little bit harder. Principal Richmond scares most of the students at Locke, but not me. He reminds me a lot of my dad.

That Dr. McKinney guy was kind of a big deal. He was a scientist, an artifacts collector, and a marine biologist. He'd discovered a sunken slave ship at the bottom of the Atlantic Ocean. He and his crew were showing us some of the valuable remains they found. It was cool to me, but most of the seventh and eighth graders in the auditorium were ready to leave. It was lunchtime for some, and third period for others.

Principal Richmond sent out another wave of instructions. "I trust that all of you are responsible enough to go wherever it is that you belong. If any of you are caught somewhere you're not supposed to be, you'll have to answer to me. That's all I'm going to say. Good afternoon."

He dismissed us, and we all took off in our own directions like shattered glass. During the crowds and craziness, I ducked off into an aisle to let the bum-rushing stream of chaos pass me up. Way at the end of the line was Pacino. He saw me, too. He came up and gave me a pound. It was like last night never happened.

"My man, Crease. What's up, Kung Fu Joe?" He gave me another pound and chopped me with his other hand across the back.

"Nothing much. You?"

Pacino was wearing the belt I'd given him. His pants were up at his waist, looking decent, not droopy.

"Hey," he said, "last night I was trippin', aiight."

I adjusted my backpack. "Yeah, cool. No big deal, man." I was kinda out of line when I'd mentioned his brother. "Carmichael wondered why you left so fast. He wanted to show you his spelling-test scores."

"Tell the little man I said what's up. Your little brother is about ten times as cool as you are!" Pacino laughed and attempted to give me some more dap. I left him hanging and shoved him a little.

The hallway was noisy, and kids were shoving.

Pacino looked around. In a hush, he said, "I gotta go to the senior building and start taking advanced placement math class." Then he shrugged and looked at me like there was something really wrong.

"Man, don't you know how crazy that is? An eighth grader taking an AP class? That's bananas, bro!" I was trying to hide the envy in my voice. My mother would go nuts if I told her I was taking a class with high school kids.

"You know I'm brilliant, baby. But that's between us, cool?"

"Cool." I gave him a jab to the gut. "I'm headed to African American history."

Pacino pulled me out of the way so other kids could pass us. "Wherever you go, watch your back. I heard something about ya boy Tariq." He was looking me dead in my eyes, completely serious.

"What did you hear? Tell me, man." The auditorium was beginning to empty, but I wasn't going to move until Pacino told me what he'd heard.

"A girl that rides the bus with one of them dudes that tried to jump you with Tariq said that he was strapped today. I think they said he had a thirty-eight, a nine or something. I don't know."

"Serious? I mean, you think I should tell somebody? You think he's gonna try something with me?" My neck started to get warm. Pacino looked worried.

"Calm down, Crease. Tariq might have something, he might not. But what you can't do is tell on him. If he's got his eyes on you, he's got his eyes on you. That's all there is to it."

"Look, I don't want to get shot today, or tomorrow, or the day after that." Now my whole face was hot.

"What did I tell you on Tuesday, huh? Didn't I say I had your back?" He stood over me with a hand on my shoulder, like a big brother.

"Yeah, but what about all of that stuff you said yesterday about me being on my own?"

"Look, that's squashed, Crease. After PSS today, I'll be there with you. Don't worry. Plenty of fools have threatened me with guns and they ended up gettin' whupped. I *got* you," he promised me. I had no choice but to trust him. He was all the backing I had. I didn't have one friend at Locke who would help me fight against Tariq Molten.

Mr. Richmond came charging up the aisle toward us. "Okay, Clapton. You've been doing better than usual, son. I'm sick of seeing your face in my office," he grumbled at Pacino.

"I'm sick of seeing your face . . . I mean . . . office, too, Mr. Richmond. You're looking at a brand-new Pacino Clapton. That's my word."

"Your word, huh?" Mr. Richmond gave Pacino a stare that didn't believe in the "new" Pacino's word. "All right. Don't let me down. You boys better get going." Mr. Richmond gave Pacino a pound and then continued his march out of the auditorium.

"Yes, sir. I won't let you down, sir," Pacino

called out. All I could do was nod, seeing how I've never had a real conversation with Principal Richmond. He and Pacino seemed like old golfing buddies from way back.

We grabbed our bags, and we headed off in separate directions. Pacino turned back toward me and said, "It'll be all right, Crease. That's my word."

I didn't say anything, just kept walking. Like Mr. Richmond, I wondered and hoped that Pacino's word was worth something. Anything at all.

2:48 P.M.
ALAIN LOCKE MIDDLE SCHOOL
THE POST-SCHOOL SUSPENSION ROOM
THE LAST DAY

She looked like a lady today. Kinda nice.

"So what's all this for, girl? I know you're not trying to step up your game or something." Pacino kept sprinkling what sounded like hidden compliments to Rosilyn. I was worried out of my mind about what Tariq would or wouldn't try to do to me after school. But for a second, I took my mind off of that and noticed Rosilyn. She did look good.

Rosilyn rolled her eyes at Pacino. She smiled at both of us. "I don't know what you're talking about, fool. I always look good. Believe that."

She twisted around and showed off her beige-and-pink skirt. She had on a pretty silk blouse and some kind of gold necklace that she must have borrowed. Her hair was pinned up, and her hoop earrings clanked every time she worked her neck at Pacino. She even smelled different, something powdery and light. She still looked skinny to me, but her skirt and the rest of her outfit really caught my attention. No lie.

"I'm just saying you never dress up like this. The welfare or child custody people must be comin' by your house this evening, right?" Pacino is always trying to crack on that girl.

"You got jokes, huh? I know you like what you see." Rosilyn sucked her teeth. "Can't a girl just decide to look extra fly out of the blue? Quit hatin'!"

"Please. Who said you looked fly? I didn't say that. Did you, Crease?" Pacino smirked at me, probably expecting me to front like he was doing.

"I didn't say it, but . . . you do look kinda sweet today, Rosilyn." I didn't know who looked more surprised, Pacino or Rosilyn.

"*Well* — I see somebody in here has got some taste. Forget you, Pacino." Rosilyn snapped her fingers like tiny firecrackers. Then she clacked her shiny brown heels back over to her workstation, put on her iPod nano, and zoned out.

Mr. Patt was on the phone. I thought he was talking to his wife because he kept saying "baby" and "honey." The filthy sixth grader Mackey didn't show up, which meant he had to make that day up and an extra one next week. Stupid sixth grader.

I don't know if Rosilyn had heard about Tariq having a gun. I turned my back on her and then leaned in closer to Pacino to ask him. "So . . . what are we gonna do?"

"Man, will you just chill? Dang! That punk got you all spooked. I shouldn't have told you."

My neck was heating up again, the fever spreading fast to my armpits. "So you were just going to let whatever is going to happen, happen?"

The only thing I kept imagining was a scene in a Bond movie with dozens of bullets flying at me. And no matter how fast I ran or how low I ducked, they would still tear through my clothes, pierce my skin, and slice my bones.

"How many times do I have to say I've got your back? He'll see me with you and turn around," Pacino bragged, like he was bulletproof. "I'm telling you, if I had your karate skills, I wouldn't be scared of anybody. Don't be an uppity mama's boy punk your whole life, Crease."

"*You're* the punk!" I yelled. Even Rosilyn heard me. She pulled one of her earbuds out and turned around.

Mr. Patt told his wife to hold on a second and then said to me, "Don't blow it or you'll be back here next week."

"I gotta be a punk or a mama's boy every time I don't say I want to knock somebody's teeth out? Or prove to you how hood I am? I'm sick of that." I was whispering, but I was heated.

"You don't need to be hood to protect yourself, fool."

"He may want to hurt me, but I won't play into that stupid stuff. I'm about using my mind, not fighting."

"Forget that!" Pacino said sharply. "Crease, those fools don't understand all of that mind and soul stuff you be poppin'. You need to tuck that in your karate bag — *brotha*."

Pacino would not give it up. He was preaching as much as Dad. "It would be cool if everybody called each other *brotha* or lived a fairy-tale life like you do, Crease, but we don't. Get over it," Pacino snapped. "If you're that scared, why don't you call one of your folks to come pick you up in one of their shiny cars?" Pacino pulled a cell phone out of his backpack and handed it to me.

"I don't want to worry them, especially if nothing's really gonna happen, right?"

I turned around to see if Rosilyn was paying attention. She wasn't. She was still listening to music, or at least I thought she was. She snatched her other earbud out, wrapped them around her iPod, then came back to Pacino's workstation.

"Look, Robeson, I can call my brothers up here. They don't like Tariq either. I'm just sayin' if you need some help or something. I know fightin' ain't one of your things." Rosilyn looked at me so pitiful when she said that, like I was a wimp.

"I'm okay, Rosilyn. Thanks anyway. It's no big deal." I tried to be cool, but it wasn't working. Now all of me was hot.

Rosilyn gently ran her fingers across my cheek. "I just don't want them to mess up that cute face."

"Here we go. The lovebirds are at it again." Pacino cracked up.

"Leave Robeson alone. He can't help it if he thinks I'm fine," Rosilyn said.

"He can have your old —" Pacino started to say something foul, I could tell. But he stopped himself. "He can have you, Rosilyn. You can run off together, get married, and have a gang of rug rats. I don't care. But what he really needs to be concerned about now is what he's gonna do when that bell rings." Pacino stopped joking. He was all serious.

The bell never got a chance to ring.

Mr. Patt said his last "baby" and "honey," then got off of his cell phone, grinning like a fat man who had just won the pancake lottery. "Good news, delinquents. I know we usually dismiss at three thirty, but I've got something important to tend to, so I'm gonna let you go early. Out."

Pacino pumped a fist. Rosilyn waved her hands in the air. I gulped extra-extra hard.

I had a mad headache that was trying to pound itself out of my temples. The inside of my mouth was sandpaper. Sweat was coming fast to my face.

I would have done anything for more time in PSS.

2:59 P.M.
MEYER BOULEVARD
PARTING WAYS

Pacino didn't want to leave me hanging. He was standing by me, slow to leave. "I was gonna ride the Metro with you if you wanted me to. Your dad has a faculty meeting or something, right?"

"Yeah, he does. But I'll be okay," I told him, not sure if I'd be okay. In the back of my mind I could see Tariq and his boys patrolling every block around the school, looking for me.

"I could go home, too. Moms is off from work today, plus she got paid, so we might go to Red Lobster or something."

"Yeah, man. Go home. I'll be okay." I chuckled a little. I was tired of telling this nut to go home to be with his mom and sisters. I put my fist out to give Pacino a pound. Instead, he gave me half dap, half hug, like you do to one of your real boys. I guess that made us official — brothas. We stood in front of the rectangular fountain on Meyer, in the center of the boulevard. There wasn't a soul in sight. Not one car came or went. It was just Pacino and me, and a strange quiet for this time of day.

Pacino reached into his backpack. "Hey, man, I almost forgot. I still have your Dad's Miles Davis." He handed me the CD.

That's when I remembered. Today was Dad's Brand New Vision meeting.

"Wanna give him the CD yourself?"

Pacino hesitated. "You mean come back to your *Cosby Show* crib?"

"Yeah, to the Huxtable house," I joked.

"Nahhh, man, I got homework. And the twins are waiting on me, and my moms, too."

"There's some guys I want you to meet, friends of my dad's. It won't take long. You can be home in time for dinner."

"I'm not meeting any preachy dudes who like listening to classical tunes."

"Answer me this, Pacino. Did you like listening to Miles?"

Pacino was slow to admit it. "Miles is cool," he said.

"These brothers are all about cool," I said.

Pacino folded his arms tight. "I'm hungry. Do these all-about-cool brothers serve snacks?"

"Leftover lasagna."

"I can work with that." He hoisted his backpack, holding on to the Miles CD. We walked to the bus stop, heading back to my house.

3:45 P.M.
BATTLEFIELD RESIDENCE
BRAND NEW VISION WEEKLY MEETING

Our family room was packed with members of an organization my dad started seven years ago called Brand New Vision. These guys go to schools and walk the streets in the worst neighborhoods to mentor boys my age and older. Pacino and I busted in as the meeting was in full swing. We practically fell on top of each other.

"You brothas will have to excuse my son and his comrade," Dad apologized to his friends.

"Sorry, Dad. Sorry, guys."

Dad introduced Pacino to the group. "Fellas, I'd like you all to meet young Pacino Clapton." Greetings came from every point in the room, in scattered, deep voices.

Pacino waved. He looked a little scared, but curious, too. He never let go of his backpack. I'm sure he wasn't expecting to come into the middle of a room filled with some of the city's most successful, highly educated, and influential men.

Mom had left the lasagna, and the BNV members were enjoying it. Pacino and I cleaned our plates before anyone else in the room. We were starvin'!

"Pacino is one of Alain Locke Middle's prize students. Am I correct?" Dad asked.

"Sure . . . I mean, yes, sir." Pacino set down his knapsack. The room was full of welcoming vibes.

A little wiry man with a gravelly voice and wide glasses, named Mr. Warren, was the first to speak to Pacino. He's the owner of a couple of bookstores in the city. He's also the father of six kids he's raising alone because his wife died. "Hey, little brotha. Keep doin' what you're doin'."

"Pacino, I would go around and introduce everyone, but that would take forever," Dad said. "If you and Robeson don't mind sitting in on the meeting, you could talk to some of the guys afterward. We don't have that much longer. We'd be honored if you stayed for the rest."

"That's cool, sir," Pacino said. He tried to sound all cool, but I could tell how excited he really was to join the group. He had sat down before my dad even asked.

I raised my hand and agreed to stick around. "Me, too, Dad. I'll stay." I slid to the back of the room. Pacino moved his bag out of the way so I could sit down. We sat at opposite ends of the fireplace. Pacino seemed ready to listen, like folks are right before the preacher gets up to deliver a sermon.

My dad stood. "Okay, let's get back to it," he said to the group. He pointed at Mr. Merle, probably the tallest member of BNV. Mr. Merle used to play pro ball back in the eighties, before the Kings moved to Sacramento. Now he has the only black-owned golf course and country club in Missouri. He's married and has two kids.

"We were about to address the school district's decision to do away with the after-school programs. What are we going to do about that, Teddy?" Mr. Merle asked my dad.

"I say we go down there, all of us, and raise some hell," Mr. Sinclair said. "There are about three hundred of us between here and St. Louis. It just isn't right. What about those parents who work late and can't get off in time to pick up their kids?" Mr. Sinclair is married and runs the Boys and Girls Club over by Cleveland Avenue.

Soon the whole room got angry. The men were tossing around their ideas all at the same time, until my dad took control of the floor.

"All right, guys, quiet down, quiet down! We can't hear any of your ideas if everyone talks at once." The group got calm in a hurry. Dad set things off by throwing out a challenge: "Forget going down there ranting and raving. Let's start our own after-school program. We can do it. Who's with me?"

"What do you mean, Battlefield?" asked Deacon Luster, the oldest deacon at our church. He must be around eighty-seven but still kickin'. He's a retired airline pilot, had been married for over fifty years, and has five kids and more than twelve grandkids. "You mean you want us to go around to the schools and watch the kids?"

"That's exactly what I mean, Deacon," Dad replied. "After all, as Sinclair has already pointed out, we're over three hundred strong."

Dad turned toward the rest of the group. "We have to stop depending on the school district, the government, and every other outside entity to look out for our children."

Pacino was watching, listening close, taking it all in. He paid special attention when Mr. Rayford, a young dude, spoke next.

"Sounds good, Mr. Battlefield, but how are we gonna reach *every* school?" Mr. Rayford works for that big J. E. Dunn Construction Company, and he's in school to be a civil engineer. He looked like a high school student to us; kinda slim, with no facial hair at all.

"I'm glad you asked," Dad said. "There are enough of us to have at least two to three members at almost every building to organize after-school activities for the kids. We can make it happen."

That was my dad's favorite saying, and his motto for the Brand New Vision group — *We can make it happen.* Everything and anything is possible to my dad if enough energy is put behind it.

"Pacino? Did you want to add something?" Dad asked. Pacino had his hand raised, but not really. Dad called him out anyway.

Pacino cleared his throat. "I just don't get it. Why do *you* or anybody else in here care about where kids go after school? It's their mama's problem, right?" Everyone got quiet then. Pacino said, "I wouldn't spend my free time running all over to help someone else's kids. I got my own little sisters to watch after school."

The whole room turned around to lay eyes on Pacino. Then they all started to talk at once. Deacon Luster tapped his cane on the floor faster than I thought his old hands could move.

Somebody yelled out, "What did that boy say?"

Dad motioned for the group to quiet down. A few men had their hands up, irritated.

Dad motioned for them to put their hands down. He said, "Pacino, you tell me. Why *should* we care?"

"That's what I'm saying. Folks have things to do, not to mention work. I know *I* have stuff to do." Pacino adjusted his jacket. "Babysitting a bunch of ungrateful kids ain't one of 'em."

"Robeson tells me you cut hair, right?" Dad asked.

"Yep. I can hook up the tightest fade you ever seen."

"Is that so?" Pacino nodded.

"Why do you do it?" Dad asked.

"Because I'm good at it, and I make a grip doin' it."

"Yeah, I know you get paid well, as smart as you are, but what do you do with the money?" Dad's gaze was all over Pacino, who sat still and answered everything thrown his way.

"I don't know. I buy clothes, kicks, DVDs. Stuff like that. But most of all, I help out my moms. Water bill, light bill, rent, whatever."

"You mean you give your mother money to pay bills and you look after your sisters? How much do you get for that? I bet you get paid, right?"

"Nope. They're my little sisters. If I don't do it, who else is gonna do it?" Pacino told Dad. He looked offended.

Another man, Mr. Wilkinson, who was new to BNV, spoke next. "What he's saying is, Does your mother have to make you stay at home and watch your little sisters? Did she *tell* you that you need to go out and make some extra money?" I didn't know Mr. Wilkinson as well as I did the other men. He was making a good point, though, and driving it home, too.

"No, she never had to ask me to do any of that stuff. It's just what I do," Pacino said. Dad walked toward Pacino.

"You don't have to do it, but your mother and your little sisters need you, and you should be proud of yourself. Are you?"

"Yeah, I guess. I never really looked at it that way."

"So what do you think would happen to your little sisters if you didn't watch after them, or if you didn't help your mother make ends meet with the bills?" Dad was right in front of Pacino now. He adjusted his glasses and folded his arms. Pacino leaned back against the fireplace.

"I guess they'd . . . I guess they'd have it bad," Pacino almost whispered as he looked to the floor.

"Hey, man, I know." Dad set his hand on Pacino's shoulder. "I grew up like you. I was the oldest. I had two little brothers, a little sister, and no dad. It was all me. I had to recognize my role, but it took me some time."

I was feeling for Pacino, too. He thought he'd only be getting leftovers and meeting some guys.

Pacino said, "Everybody here seems so important and so busy. When do you find the time to help anybody else?"

"You're not the only one with family members to look after. All of the men in here have positions ranging from janitors to judges. We've got fathers, grandfathers, husbands, single guys, you name it. But none of that matters. We *find* the time because we care about our community. Who's gonna do it if we don't?" Mr. Wilkinson added.

Pacino played with the zipper on his jacket.

Dad walked over to the couch and picked up his leather satchel. He pulled out two sheets of paper and handed them to Pacino and me. "Check this out. This is the Brand New Vision mission statement, or creed, or preamble. Every man in this room has committed to bettering the lives of young men and making themselves visible in the community. They've memorized every word on this paper. We live by it. I want you to do the same."

"You want me to memorize this?" Pacino asked, with the paper in his hand, but his arm was still stuck in the air, like he wanted to pass it back to Dad. I took mine and scanned over it really fast. It wasn't new to me. I was in Dad's office the day he wrote it. The group recites the preamble together before each meeting.

"What's the problem, Mr. Straight A's? The next time I see you I want you to hit me with it, word for word. I'm sure your buddy Robeson here will help you with that. Cool?" Dad threw out the challenge to Pacino.

"Cool. No problem, Mr. Battlefield." Pacino folded the paper in half and slid it in his jacket pocket — his way of accepting the challenge.

Mr. Caruthers stood up and asked my dad, "Hey, Teddy, did I hear the little brotha say he could cut the tightest fade you've ever seen?" Mr. Caruthers owns five barbershops and a chain of all-natural beauty supply stores. "Pacino, if you come to one of my shops, I'll let you check out some real artists, show you how it's done."

"Are you serious?" Pacino asked. "I bought all of my equipment from your supply shop on Troost."

"It's settled, then. I'll give you one of my cards and you ask your folks if it's okay," Caruthers said. It was the first time I had ever seen Pacino with awe on his face.

"Thanks, sir." Pacino shook Mr. Caruthers's hand and stuffed the card in his pocket. He had that look in his eyes. I had seen it a few times before when other boys had sat in on meetings. I could tell that being around all of these men changed the way he thought about a few things, if only for one night.

My dad stood before all of the BNV members and said, "Thanks to all of you for coming. We'll discuss the next steps to take on the after-school program in the upcoming days." Then he closed the meeting like he always does. "Let's move forward with power and purpose, men. May God continue to bless you all so that you may bless others. Good afternoon."

TROUBLE
ON
FRIDAY

3:13 P.M.
63RD AND INDIANA
THE SETUP

After school, I walked past Locke Senior High's football field, which runs adjacent to Indiana the entire length of the 64th and 65th blocks. The football team was about to start practice.

No more PSS. This was the first evening this week when I'd be headed home straight after school. Dad had another faculty meeting at work, so he couldn't pick me up this evening, either. I had to catch the Metro.

Halfway to 63rd Street, I remembered that I had seen Pacino earlier in the day and promised to meet him at the fountain on Meyer Boulevard at three thirty. My dad wanted me to give him two more Miles Davis CDs to keep. Dad always says the three things we should never hesitate to give away are good books, good music, and good advice.

When I turned around to head back toward the fountain, I tripped hard on the jacked-up concrete and fell to the sidewalk. When I looked up, there were Poke and Chauncey, Tariq's boys.

"You just can't stay on your feet, can you? That's the second time this week that I've knocked you on your butt, boy," Poke, the lanky one, said.

Chauncey, the cocky kid, barked, "Get up, fool." He'd gotten his cornrows redone. They didn't look so ragged anymore. "Get up, fool," Chauncey repeated. "We ain't gonna do nothing."

"You looking crazy, man. You running from somebody?" Poke asked. He readjusted the shoulder pads and football helmet he was carrying on his back.

Chauncey dropped his football gear to his feet. Then he gripped one of my hands and yanked me up.

"Nah, I'm cool," I answered. "Where are you guys . . . I mean . . . what do you want?"

Poke said, "Man, we don't want anything from you. *You* ran into *us*."

I bit my lip. "I'm saying . . . the other day, the both of you and Tariq were going to . . . I didn't know what you were going to do." I braced myself and held up my clenched fists. "But I ain't no punk. Let's get it over with."

They paused and then gawked down on me like I was a silly alien boy from the planet What's-His-Problem.

"Put your hands down, boy!" Chauncey slapped both of my fists toward the ground. "We don't have a problem with you."

Poke said, "Speak for yourself, Chauncey. I wanna slap the taste out of his funny-looking mouth!" Poke threw his football equipment down and pushed his lanky elbows and tight knuckles up to the sky. Then he started laughing. "Nah, I was just messin' with you, man. You aiight."

Chauncey said, "Yeah, Battlefield. Soon as we found out who you was related to, that changed everything. For real."

"Who am I related to?"

Chauncey said, "Your pops. Mr. Battlefield. I owe him a lot."

"Me, too," added Poke. "If it wasn't for him, I don't know where we'd be. I'd probably have a room at that halfway house, group-home shack where Tariq lives."

"How do y'all know my dad?"

Chauncey ran down how he met Dad. "He rolled up on our block last year by himself. I think he was on his way around the corner from where we live to tutor some kids at the Genesis School. Something like that. I don't remember. We were about to scrap with somebody. I forgot who it was. Your pops jumped out of his car like he was the cops or something. Then he just broke us up."

Poke jumped in. "I remember that. First of all, he was lucky nobody jacked him for his ride, plus he was in the wrong hood to be playin' hero. Forty-fifth and South Benton? We thought he was crazy. But he did it anyway."

My dad is almost *crazy*-brave, but he'd never told me about stopping a fight on 45th and South Benton. "Yeah? What happened then?"

"Your dad started talkin' about why we shouldn't be fightin' and how he had just seen a police car around the corner," Chauncey said.

Poke jumped in again. "He said they'd take our black butts to jail just for being in the streets, and he knew that our parents didn't have money for bail. We cracked up at that 'cause he was right!"

"We respected him and squashed everything.

It took a lot of guts to do what he did. Then he stuck around and started telling us about the history of our neighborhood and all of the black city leaders that were from our part of town." Chauncey looked over at Poke because he knew he was about to be interrupted again. But Poke let Chauncey continue.

"On top of all of that, he gave us some free passes to a basketball game at the Sprint Center and some flyers about his organization, called BNV. He said we could come by the new youth center on Clever Boulevard anytime in the evening. So we did."

Poke busted in. "And that's where we met Coach Thornton. We transferred from Central to Locke just to be on the JV football team."

Chauncey looked at me and said, "Hey, if your pops is that cool, we figured his son can't be that bad. Plus, Tariq is crazy. We've known him since he was in the first grade. I thought he just wanted to punk you in the stairs the other day. Not really do anything, just scare you. I've kinda chilled out on all that fighting for no stupid reason. I wasn't gonna get in trouble for that fool."

Turned out these guys were cool. I wasn't so scared of them now.

"Yeah, it was stupid," I told them. But I still had an eye out for Tariq. "Where is he now? Did you hear that he had a gun today?"

Poke cut a look to Chauncey. "Oh yeah. He did. I saw it myself. But I'm done with that chump. Tariq ain't nothing but trouble. I mean, I ain't got no problem roughing up somebody, but Tariq is on some wild ride, and that ain't me."

Chauncey picked up his football gear off of the sidewalk. "But on the real, you don't have to worry about Tariq messin' with you. He's after some other dude, like *for real, for real* after this dude."

I didn't even ask why Tariq wasn't after me anymore. Poke and Chauncey were about to cross the street and cut through a gap in a chain-link fence. They were running late to practice. I asked, "Why is he after that other dude?"

"They just don't get along, so Tariq said he's gonna take care of it. That's all I know," Poke said before he eyed a slit in the fence across the street for him to slide his skinny frame through.

"C'mon, man, tell me — who's on Tariq's hit list?" I asked.

"As long as it ain't you, just stay away from Tariq," Chauncey answered.

But it was Poke who gave it up. "The kid's name is P-something. Pacheeko or something crazy like that."

Chauncey bumped me. "We gotta go, Battlefield. Get off of these streets, boy." The two of them took off toward practice.

That's when the wrecking ball hit me. Everything stopped. My brain shut down immediately. My body took over. I just started running. I ran like a genetically engineered track star. The 64th and 65th blocks of Indiana became a blur of bushes and mail boxes.

The front lawn of the senior building is the length of a football field. I don't think my feet even touched the ground. I cleared it in seconds. What would I do when I got there? Would I be too late?

The fountain.

When I got to the fountain, Pacino was there — and so was Tariq.

3:22 P.M.
MEYER BOULEVARD
THE FOUNTAIN

Tariq was at the edge of the fountain, holding a small gun to Pacino's chest. They looked like statues. Neither one of them spoke or moved. Their reflections danced back and forth on the water.

Tariq turned around and saw me. I'd startled him. "Look who's here. You just can't stay away from trouble, can you?" The arm that he held the gun up with started to shake a little bit. He looked back at Pacino, then smiled like he had just landed a two-for-one deal. "You must be the most unluckiest fool ever."

Pacino looked at me but didn't say a word. He blinked, licked his lips. He was wearing his gray-and-blue Royals cap, cocked to the back. His arms were at his sides, his bag at his feet. He looked calmer than Tariq did.

"I was just . . . I was just . . . on my way home and . . ." I stuttered.

Tariq spoke slowly, carefully. "You don't live over here. You're too white-bread to live on this side of the fountain."

"I was meeting —"

"Unless you wanna see this dude get lit up, you need to keep movin'." Tariq pressed the gun deeper into Pacino's chest.

"I can't do that. Why don't you just . . . put the gun away, man?"

"I ain't saying it no more. Leave!" He grabbed Pacino by the collar, then pointed the gun at me with the other hand. I dropped my bag.

"Go 'head, man. Leave like he said, Crease!" Pacino was wincing, pleading.

Tariq looked back and forth between us. "Crease, is this your girlfriend or something?" Tariq was crazy with that gun, shaking it and looking scared and wild, too. "I got enough slugs in here for the both of you."

I lowered my head, dropped my hands to my side, and closed my eyes. If I was going to get shot, I didn't want to see it.

"What are you doing, praying?" he asked. "I don't know why you wasting your time praying.

You're about to talk to God face-to-face in a minute." This was a joke to Tariq, a game.

Finally, Pacino spoke. "He ain't done nothing to you, you little punk. Leave him alone."

My eyes were still closed. I tried to take my mind to another place. I was almost wishing something would happen to get this over with.

That's when I heard Dad's BNV credo: *We can make it happen.* When I opened my eyes, Pacino was swinging at Tariq. Tariq jerked back, avoiding the punch, but he still had a tight grip around Pacino's neck. "What was that, huh?" He swung the gun like a sling blade and opened up the right side of Pacino's face. Blood escaped down Pacino's cheek, onto his clothes and the ground.

His head slumped, but somehow he was still on his feet. Tariq took one look at me and said, "This one is for you." Then he reached all the way back, like he was swinging a pickax, and came down with the butt of the gun smack dead between Pacino's eyes. It was like lightning struck his forehead. His cap flew off of his head and spun like a helicopter seed into the fountain. The blow was enough to drop him to his knees and finally flat to the pavement.

Tariq turned to me then. "You know — I never did like you," he said.

The BNV credo was a siren in my head: *We can make it happen.* Just as loud as my thoughts were the ways of kyokushin.

Disarming somebody with a weapon was one of the first things I learned when I started studying kyokushin. It would've been easy to do with Tariq, but he was too far away from me and he was about to go off on some messed-up rampage.

He started laughing all loud. "Look at you baby fools." He couldn't stop cracking up. "You look like you're about to pee in your diapers. I don't need bullets to lay you out. You just two soft, sissy-made punks."

Right then, Tariq pulled the pistol's trigger three times fast — *click*, *click*, *click*. I *did* nearly wet my pants but saw right off that the gun wasn't loaded.

I looked over and was surprised to see Pacino slowly rising to his feet, wet, still spitting blood, and wiping his face. He just wouldn't stay down.

We can make it happen.

Tariq came running at me with the gun over

his head. Pacino lunged in to help me. "Crease!" he shouted, grabbing Tariq. The gun flew from Tariq's hand. He stopped, his eyes got wide. He knew he was about to get it.

Tariq swung out a weak punch, first at Pacino, then at me. I blocked it and then gave him a knife-hand to the neck. He was bent over, gagging, gasping, finding his balance. That's when I grabbed the back of his head with both hands and came up with a strong knee kick, first to his nose, then mouth and head. He fell backward and smacked hard to the pavement.

I kept kicking until I felt Tariq's warm blood on my pants leg.

When I finally let up, my knee was numb and tingling. Tariq staggered onto his feet, blowing blood and spit. He tried to come at me but couldn't. He was confused, like a drunk who couldn't make sense of stuff that was happening too fast. He tripped backward and stayed down, half conscious, half struggling.

My heart felt like it was a hundred pounds. Pacino grabbed the gun, then came to me. He was still bleeding from his head and face. "You all right, Crease?" I didn't answer. I *couldn't* answer. I couldn't stop crying.

I was no different from Tariq for what I had done to him. Yeah, Tariq hadn't given me much of a choice, but I'd slammed everything I stood for. I tried to bite down on the crying, but it was holding on. The worst part was that I wanted to give Tariq another kick. Tariq was down for good, though. Pacino walked me slowly to the edge of the fountain, where we sat. "Thanks, brother" was all he said.

Cars began to circle the fountain. Then people started showing up, running to help.

A lady with two Labradors took off her jacket and covered Tariq with it. A girl hopped off her bike and offered her coat to Pacino. The lady with the dogs asked me, "Baby, are you okay? How did all of this happen?" I wiped my nose with my sleeve, still not ready to speak.

5:48 P.M.
RESEARCH MEDICAL CENTER
WAITING ROOM

"Robeson, look at me when I talk to you."

But I couldn't lift my eyes to Dad's, not even briefly.

It was Mr. Wilkinson, Dad's friend from BNV, who got me to look up. I knew he was a policeman, but I'd never seen him in uniform. "Robeson, I'm going to have to ask you some questions. Tariq's hurt badly, and we need your help."

The hospital hallway was busy with other policemen, nurses, families, announcements flying out of a loudspeaker, and us.

Pacino had been taken to another room. When we got to the hospital in a police car, they refused to keep us together, even though we'd told the police that we *were* together — that it wasn't us fighting against each other.

Tariq had been put into an ambulance at the fountain, and I had no idea what had happened to him after that.

Mr. Wilkinson lifted my chin. He wouldn't let me escape his gaze.

"Robeson, I'm what they call a youth aid investigator. I'll be handling things along with another investigator who's been in the Juvenile Investigation Unit for over twenty years. He's worked with the parole officer of that Tariq Molten kid many times."

Dad was inspecting my shirt, which was covered with blood specks. He hugged me.

"Does Mom know?" I asked.

"She's flying back from Maryland now."

I asked Mr. Wilkinson, "How are Pacino and Tariq doing?"

"Pacino's fine. He's given us some of the details we need. They're going to keep him overnight for observation, but he's in good shape." I wasn't expecting the news on Tariq to be good, though. Usually, people give the worse of two pieces of news last. I was right.

"Tariq's situation is a little bit trickier. He's fading in and out of consciousness." Mr. Wilkinson was relaying to us what the doctors had told him. There was worry in his voice. "Tariq's nose is broken, and he's suffered a grade-three concussion."

"Will he be okay?"

"The doctors said that he'll more than likely suffer some serious memory loss when he wakes up," Mr. Wilkinson said.

I was so scared, I let out a breath.

Mr. Wilkinson said, "The paramedics got there just in time. A couple more minutes and Tariq wouldn't have made it." Mr. Wilkinson shook his head. "The good Lord was with you fellas today, Robeson."

"I've been praying all afternoon," Dad said.

Mr. Wilkinson jumped in. "That's another thing, Robeson. We found the gun by the fountain. It was stolen and it had Tariq's prints all over it. And there was a witness who saw him holding it on you and your friend."

Dad said, "I don't even want to imagine what would have happened if the gun was loaded." I was ready for Dad to tell me I was no longer a Battlefield, that I didn't deserve to keep our family name. And I knew a lecture was coming. But Dad was more concerned with me, Tariq, and Pacino. "Sometimes in life, Robeson, you do what a situation calls for. You may surprise yourself and react in a way that you never knew you were capable of. I'm just glad you're safe." Dad hugged me again.

"Your father is right, Robeson. Your friend Pacino is on the third floor with his family, waiting to tell you thanks." Mr. Wilkinson jabbed me in the arm, like Pacino does.

"What about Tariq?" I asked.

"The boy's got no family to speak of. We called his grandparents, but no one answered. We even called the group home where he lives, but nobody's shown up yet. He's by himself."

6:07 P.M.
RESEARCH MEDICAL CENTER
PACINO'S ROOM

Mr. Wilkinson showed me and Dad to where Pacino was on the third floor. Pacino's mom welcomed us as soon as we arrived in the room where they were keeping an eye on Pacino overnight. He had a huge knot on his forehead and the right side of his face was bandaged. Other than that, he looked fine.

"You must be Crease. Come on in, baby. I'm Ms. Clapton, Pacino's mama, but everybody calls me Missy." She hugged Dad and me like we were family. Dad hugged her back, just like he does to his sister, my aunt Vanessa, when it looks like she really needs a nice strong hug. "I've heard so much about you both, good stuff, too. Find a seat somewhere."

For a woman who works two jobs, she greeted us with a wave of energy. She looked anything but tired. She had eyelashes like a movie star, and her almond eyes were a shade of brown that I had never seen. But her warm smile was something that I see every single day of my life — it was like my own mother's.

The Clapton family had really come ahead for Pacino. There were already flowers and get-well cards in the room.

Pacino's twin sisters and four other kids were watching *SpongeBob* on the TV hanging in the corner of the room.

Ms. Clapton and I were able to ease through the crowded room of family members to stand next to Pacino's bed. Dad found it harder to squeeze through. He just stood at the door and held a conversation with one of the men in the room. I think it was an uncle or cousin. I recognized him from the wall of pictures at Pacino's apartment.

"Look, I just want to tell you thanks, Crease. Really, baby," Ms. Clapton said.

"No problem, Ms. Clapton. He would have done the same thing for me."

Pacino was sitting up in the bed. He was glad to see me and Dad. As I leaned in closer, I noticed that his right eye was swollen a little. Dried blood spots were seeping through his bandages.

I leaned close and spoke quickly. "Pacino. It's me. It's Crease, man."

"Man, what are you whispering for? I ain't dying, fool." Pacino moaned, but he was smiling, too. He held a hand up and I grabbed it, squeezed it tight. He was going to be okay. I felt it in his grip.

"Same old Pacino. Boy, you better be glad I showed up to save your sorry butt," I joked with him.

"Saved me? Somebody told you wrong, Crease. Nobody needs to save me. Ya dig?" He closed his eyes and winced.

"Just lay back, man." I helped him recline a little.

Pacino's mother handed him a cup of ice water. "Man, can you tell my moms that men like us need *food*? I'm hungry! They got some fries to go with that water? I got the taste for a beef on bun barbecue sandwich, too."

"And some slaw," I added.

"And some baked beans. Crease, hand me my jacket and shoes. We getting out of here."

We both cracked up. Pacino looked tired.

"Hey, man, rest," I said. "Tomorrow evening, my dad and I can bring you some grub."

"I'm getting out of here in the morning. I'm cool, Crease. I guess I can live on hospital food for one night."

Dad left the room to answer a call. Pacino's mother was busy with the twins.

Pacino asked, "So where is your boy Tariq? I bet the cops got him all hemmed up."

"No, man, he's right here in this hospital."

Pacino said, "Tell the nurse to give my hospital food to *him*." We both laughed.

"I got your back," I said. "You've had mine all week, so I owe you."

Pacino said, "Man, you've been tough enough today. Save your fight for the streets." I gave Pacino a pound, and we laughed together again. I didn't care anymore if he thought I was tough enough or hard enough or cool enough. All I knew was that when it mattered most, I was *friend* enough.

"You need anything? Looks like more people are coming in. I better go," I said to Pacino.

"I'm cool. I'm cool. Go 'head, man. Tell your dad that I was wearing a belt when all of this stuff went down. At least I looked presentable when I got bashed in the face, right?" He laughed at his own joke.

I chuckled a little and said, "You can keep the belt."

"Thanks. I owe you, huh?" he said before he took a bite out of the hospital hamburger on his tray and then spit it right back out.

I thought about everything that happened earlier and said, "Nah, you don't owe me anything, Pacino. Just get better. That's all."

He didn't owe me a thing. We were boys.

SOLUTIONS
ON
SATURDAY

11:00 A.M.
RESEARCH MEDICAL CENTER
TARIQ'S ROOM

Dad and I went back to the hospital the next day to visit Pacino and to check out the situation with Tariq.

Pacino was in his room with his mom, packing to go home. He looked good. He and the twins were playing cards and laughing.

"Hey, Pacino, I brought you some of my mom's mousse cake."

"Thanks, man." Pacino was definitely feeling better. He sliced off some of the cake to share with the twins and ate the rest quickly.

"Hey, I'm outta here," he said. "See you at Locke on Monday."

"But not in PSS."

Pacino bumped me. "You know it."

Mr. Wilkinson was in the hall. He'd already been at the hospital when we arrived. When I left

Pacino's room, I asked, "What's gonna happen to Tariq?"

"More than likely, he'll end up at the Boonville Correctional Center. They all do."

I asked, "Can I go into his room?"

Mr. Wilkinson motioned to Dad and me to follow him.

The blinds were closed. There were no teddy bears holding balloons, no flowers, no TV high in the corner, entertaining visitors. The room was empty of laughter. No visitors, family, or friends. There was only silence.

Tariq's breathing was slow, hard. The room was quiet and thick with the weight of a kid who had nobody. That's when an idea came ahead faster than I could catch it spilling from my mouth.

"Dad, there has to be one of the Brand New Vision members who can help Tariq. Maybe *we* can do something." I don't know where this idea came from — it flew in like a plane I wasn't expecting to see above my head.

"Robeson, I've helped all kinds of kids just like Tariq. But I've never reached out to one who could have killed one of my very own kids. That's where I draw the line."

"Dad, you tell me all the time about how the jails are filled with *us*. Well, here's one we can keep out. Tariq's no different."

Mr. Wilkinson was already working on it. "You remember Sergio Steele? He used to play college football and then went pro about twelve, thirteen years ago," he said to Dad.

Dad was quick to answer. "He came with you and a couple of other new BNV members last month, right?"

"Right. And his brother-in-law was telling me last week that he and Sergio have a hundred-and-forty-acre ranch in Nicodemus, Kansas, for young brothers, homeless, abused, in trouble with the law, bad luck, whatever. It's been operating for almost a year now," Mr. Wilkinson said. He was all pumped up about the possibilities. "I'll step outside and give him a call right now. I'll handle this case myself, Teddy. You can count on me. Back in a minute." He jetted out the door.

"I'm going out here with Mike to see what I can do to help out. You gonna be okay?" Dad asked me.

"Yeah, Dad, I'm cool. Go 'head," I responded with confidence.

Before he left the room, he gave me a hug and held it for a few seconds. It wasn't a half pound-half hug. It was a real type of hug; the type that fathers give to their sons; the type that men give to someone who they really respect.

He looked at me and whispered, "Thank you, son." I didn't say anything. I just hugged him back. He turned and started to walk out of the room again but slower, his shoulders broad, his head high; he turned on that strong Battlefield swagger I hoped to perfect someday.

I walked over to Tariq's bedside. His nose was fitted with a brace. His face was still swollen. Just for a second, I could have sworn he opened his eyes and looked straight at me. I pulled up a chair and sat next to the bed. I became his only visitor.

The nurse who had been in Pacino's room tipped her head in the door and said, "Making your rounds, huh?"

"I'll get out of your way soon," I replied.

"No, it's okay. I'll come back. These boys have a real good friend in you."

I scooted my chair as close as I could get it to his bedside. And right then, it hit me, something Dad had told me earlier.

Sometimes we do what the situation calls for and end up surprising ourselves. I don't know what came over me; maybe it was my parents whispering to me all of the lessons they've learned about forgiveness.

I stood up, held my head high, placed one hand on the bed, and began to recite the BNV preamble. With each line, I could see images of everything that had occurred over the past three days. At that point, my father's words had become my own:

"We are the protectors. We are leaders in our communities, in our neighborhoods, in our families and homes. We will use our knowledge, our experiences, our wisdom, and strength to help improve the lives of those in need of encouragement, compassion, and direction. We will make ourselves visible and set good examples of what real men should be. I will uphold this responsibility with every fiber of my being. Future generations are depending on me, on us.

"Am I my brother's keeper?"

And before I could answer that question to complete the last line of the preamble, I glanced toward the door, and to my surprise, there was Pacino. I was so relieved to see him. I'd spent the whole night before wondering if he'd be okay. Even seeing him earlier made me wonder — and worry.

Pacino looked at me, smiled, and then recited the last line of the preamble on his own. *"I most certainly am, and will continue to be, with sincerity, with determination, and love."*

Slowly, he turned and walked away, back toward his own room. He'd found the time to memorize the preamble, which showed me he still had his memory. And he had set aside whatever beef he had with Tariq. I could see in his eyes that he understood where I was coming from. We had made a connection, like brothers do.

Real brothers.

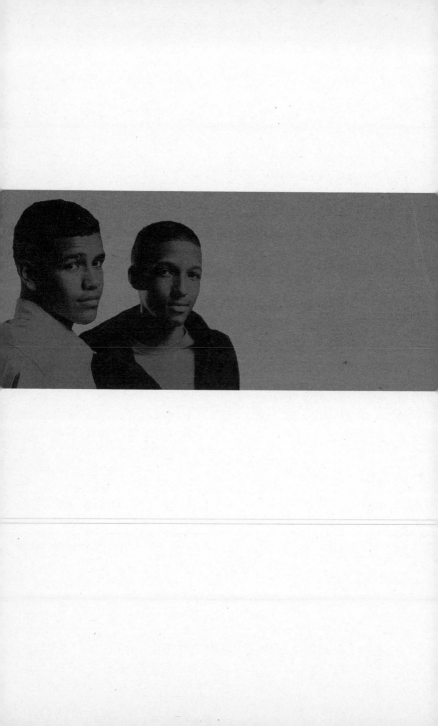

BROTHERS

10:40 A.M.
ARROWHEAD STADIUM

"Now, aren't you glad we stopped and picked up that hat and scarf, boy? You were gonna freeze your butt off if we hadn't." Dad jabbed at Pacino from the driver's seat. We pulled into the jammed parking lot of Arrowhead Stadium behind a train of other cars filled with Chiefs fans.

"I don't care how cold it is. I would've come here shirtless with paint all over my body like one of those crazy fans," Pacino answered.

It was three months after the fountain incident. Pacino's headaches were gone. The stitches were out. We barely talked about that day with Tariq. I think we had both moved on, especially since Tariq had gone off to the boys' ranch in Nicodemus. Plus, I heard that he'd made a full recovery. I was really relieved about that.

"Yeah, and you would've caught pneumonia like one of those crazy fans," I told Pacino.

"I don't mind getting sick if my team can pull off a big win against the Chargers today. We'll win the division, get home-field advantage, sweep everybody, and finish out December at thirteen and two. *I'll take a nice hot case of pneumonia, please.*" Pacino held up a finger and ordered as if he was at a restaurant. Carmichael was sitting in the backseat with me, cracking up at Pacino.

Dad laughed, too.

We were about six cars back from the pay booth. Dad looked ahead at the price posted up and said, "Twenty-five dollars? That's robbery. But I guess as long as the Chiefs are winning, these diehard fans will pay it." Dad always complains about the high price even though parking passes come with his season tickets package.

"So the whole gang is here, huh, Daddy?" Carmichael asked.

"The Battlefields," Dad said.

"And a special guest," Pacino said.

"You're no *guest*. You come over so much now, it's like you're one of my big-headed boys," Dad responded to Pacino, calling him one of his sons in a roundabout way.

"This is my first time being at an NFL stadium. I appreciate this, man. Really," Pacino said. "I'm just surprised Crease picked me over Rosilyn."

I said, "Yeah, so what. She's my new girl. You're just jealous, fool."

Dad and Carmichael started making kissing sounds.

Inside the stadium, before we made it to our seats, we picked up beef on bun sandwiches, a platter of ribs, baked beans, and fries. Carmichael got to the food first. Before he finished off all the fries, Pacino snatched up the last three. "Save some for your older brothers."

Pacino passed one fry to Dad, one to me, and grubbed on the third.

I had to go stand in the extra-long line that had formed for the restroom so I told them to go ahead without me.

"You better hurry up, man. You're gonna miss kickoff. We don't have TiVo out here!" Pacino yelled out.

"Yeah, son, we can't have fun without you," Dad chimed in.

"Take your time, Robeson. He'll be my big brother until you get back," Carmichael said as he looked up toward Pacino.

"Man, even when Crease gets back from the john, I'll still be your big brother. Nothing wrong with having two, right?" Pacino asked before he put Carmichael in a headlock.

Carmichael laughed, "No! No! Now let me go! Let me go!"

As I watched all three of them walk away, I thought about how sometimes things can really turn out pretty good when you stick to what you believe in.

DERRICK BARNES is the author of several acclaimed books, including *The Making of Dr. Truelove*, which was an ALA Quick Picks selection and has been hailed by the New York Public Library as one of the 100 Best Books for the Teen Age. Derrick and his wife, Tinka, reside in Kansas City, Missouri, with their three sons.